GRAND
TOUR

ETERNITY NOW: VOLUME 3

GRAND TOUR

LUKE
ACTS

NET

THOMAS NELSON
Since 1798

www.ThomasNelson.com

NET NT Series Eternity Now: *Volume 3: Grand Tour*

Copyright © 2022 by Thomas Nelson, a division of HarperCollins Christian Publishing, Inc.

Published in Nashville, Tennessee, by Thomas Nelson. Thomas Nelson is a registered trademark of HarperCollins Christian Publishing, Inc.

The NET Bible, New English Translation
Copyright © 1996, 2019 by Biblical Studies Press, LLC

NET Bible® is a registered trademark.

For free access to the NET Bible, the complete set of 60,000 translators' notes, and Bible study resources, visit:

    bible.org
    netbible.org
    netbible.com

Used by permission. All rights reserved.

Library of Congress Control Number: 2021952031

This Bible was set in the Thomas Nelson NET Typeface, created at the 2K/DENMARK A/S type foundry.

All rights reserved.

Printed in the United States of America

22 23 24 25 25 27 28 29 30 / TRM / 10 9 8 7 6 5 4 3 2 1

CONTENTS

TO THE READER

AN INTRODUCTION TO THE NEW ENGLISH TRANSLATION

You have been born anew ... through the living and enduring word of God.
1 Peter 1:23

The New English Translation (NET) is the newest complete translation of the original biblical languages into English. In 1995 a multidenominational team of more than twenty-five of the world's foremost biblical scholars gathered around the shared vision of creating an English Bible translation that could overcome old challenges and boldly open the door for new possibilities. The translators completed the first edition in 2001 and incorporated revisions based on scholarly and user feedback in 2003 and 2005. In 2019 a major update reached its final stages. The NET's unique translation process has yielded a beautiful, faithful English Bible for the worldwide church today.

What sets the NET Bible apart from other translations? We encourage you to read the full story of the NET's development and additional details about its translation philosophy at netbible.com/net-bible-preface. But we would like to draw your attention to a few features that commend the NET to all readers of the Word.

TRANSPARENT AND ACCOUNTABLE

Have you ever wished you could look over a Bible translator's shoulder as he or she worked?

Bible translation usually happens behind closed doors—few outside the translation committee see the complex decisions underlying the words that appear in their English Bibles. Fewer still have the opportunity to review and speak into the translators' decisions.

Throughout the NET's translation process, every working draft was made publicly available on the Internet. Bible scholars, ministers, and laypersons from around the world logged millions of review sessions. No other translation is so openly accountable to the worldwide church or has been so thoroughly vetted.

And yet the ultimate accountability was to the biblical text itself. The NET Bible is neither crowdsourced nor a "translation by consensus." Rather, the NET translators filtered every question and suggestion through the very best insights from biblical linguistics, textual criticism, and their unswerving commitment to following the text wherever it leads. Thus, the NET remains supremely accurate and trustworthy while also benefiting from extensive review by those who would be reading, studying, and teaching from its pages.

BEYOND THE "READABLE VS. ACCURATE" DIVIDE

The uniquely transparent and accountable translation process of the NET has been crystallized in the most extensive set of Bible translators' notes ever created. More than 60,000 notes highlight every major decision, outline alternative views, and explain difficult or nontraditional renderings. Freely available at netbible.org and in print in the *NET Bible, Full Notes Edition*, these notes help the NET overcome one of the biggest challenges facing any Bible translation: the tension between *accuracy* and *readability*.

If you have spent more than a few minutes researching the English version of the Bible, you have probably encountered a "translation spectrum"—a simple chart with the most wooden-but-precise translations and paraphrases on the far left (representing a "word-for-word" translation approach) and the loosest-but-easiest-to-read translations and paraphrases on the far right (representing a "thought-for-thought" philosophy of translation). Some translations intentionally lean toward one end of the spectrum or the other, embracing the strengths and weaknesses of their chosen approach. Most try to strike a balance between the extremes, weighing accuracy against readability—striving to reflect the grammar of the underlying biblical languages while still achieving acceptable English style.

But the NET moves beyond that old dichotomy. Because of the extensive translators' notes, the NET never has to compromise. Whenever faced with a difficult translation choice, the translators were free to put the strongest option in the main text while documenting the challenge, their thought process, and the solution in the notes.

The benefit to you, the reader? You can be sure that the NET is a translation you can trust—nothing has been lost in translation or obscured by a translator's dilemma. Instead, you are invited to see for yourself and gain the kind of transparent access to the biblical languages previously available only to scholars.

MINISTRY FIRST

One more reason to love the NET: Modern Bible translations are typically copyrighted, posing a challenge for ministries hoping to quote more than a few passages in their Bible study resources, curriculum, or other programming. But the NET is for everyone, with "ministry first" copyright innovations that encourage ministries to quote and share the life-changing message of Scripture as freely as possible. In fact, one of the major motivations behind the creation of the NET was the desire to ensure that ministries had un-fettered access to a top-quality modern Bible translation without needing to embark on a complicated process of securing permissions.

Visit netbible.com/net-bible-copyright to learn more.

TAKE UP AND READ

With its balanced, easy-to-understand English text and a transparent translation process that invites you to see for yourself the richness of the biblical languages, the NET is a Bible you can embrace as your own. Clear, readable, elegant, and accurate, the NET presents Scripture as meaningfully and powerfully today as when these words were first communicated to the people of God.

Our prayer is that the NET will be a fresh and exciting invitation to you—and Bible readers everywhere—to "let the word of Christ dwell in you richly" (Col 3:16).

The Publishers

LUKE

PROLOGUE

Luke was a local doctor. If there was one thing he could not be as a physician, it was careless. Lives depended on it. Even the smallest of details mattered as he treated the ill and injured each day. The second quality he needed was compassion. Patients are more than physical problems to be cured. They are people who want to be made well *and* cared for.

When it came to telling Jesus' story, Luke used both the compassion and conscientiousness that made him a good doctor. He needed to get the facts straight. He needed to provide as many details of Jesus' life, ministry, death, and resurrection as he could. There could be no doubt that what he shared was true.

At the same time, he needed to help people see the human side of it all. Not just the human side of Jesus, God in the flesh, but the humanity of the very ones Jesus had come for too. Jesus had not brought salvation for nameless, faceless people. He had come not for the masses, but for individuals. He had come to care for people: For men and women. For children. For the rich and the poor. For the Jews, Romans, Greeks, and all of the world. Jesus was the great physician who had come to seek and save the lost no matter who they might be. That was his heart for people then, and it is still his heart for people today.

CHAPTER 1

EXPLANATORY PREFACE

Now many have undertaken to compile an account of the things that have been fulfilled among us, like the accounts passed on to us by those who were eyewitnesses and servants of the word from the beginning. So it seemed good to me as well, because I have followed all things carefully from the beginning, to write an orderly account for you, most excellent Theophilus, so that you may know for certain the things you were taught.

BIRTH ANNOUNCEMENT OF JOHN THE BAPTIST

During the reign of Herod king of Judea, there lived a priest named Zechariah who belonged to the priestly division of Abijah, and he had a wife named Elizabeth, who was a descendant of Aaron. They were both righteous in the sight of God, following all the commandments and ordinances of the Lord blamelessly.

But they did not have a child because Elizabeth was barren, and they were both very old.

Now while Zechariah was serving as priest before God when his division was on duty, he was chosen by lot, according to the custom of the priesthood, to enter the Holy Place of the Lord and burn incense. Now the whole crowd of people were praying outside at the hour of the incense offering. An angel of the Lord, standing on the right side of the altar of incense, appeared to him. And Zechariah, visibly shaken when he saw the angel, was seized with fear. But the angel said to him, "Do not be afraid, Zechariah, for your prayer has been heard, and your wife Elizabeth will bear you a son; you will name him John. Joy and gladness will come to you, and many will rejoice at his birth, for he will be great in the sight of the Lord. He must never drink wine or strong drink, and he will be filled with the Holy Spirit, even before his birth. He will turn many of the people of Israel to the Lord their God. And he will go as forerunner before the Lord in the spirit and power of Elijah, to turn the hearts of the fathers back to their children and the disobedient to the wisdom of the just, to make ready for the Lord a people prepared for him."

Zechariah said to the angel, "How can I be sure of this? For I am an old man, and my wife is old as well." The angel answered him, "I am Gabriel, who stands in the presence of God, and I was sent to speak to you and to bring you this good news. And now because you did not believe my words, which will be fulfilled in their time, you will be silent, unable to speak, until the day these things take place."

Now the people were waiting for Zechariah, and they began to wonder why he was delayed in the Holy Place. When he came out, he was not able to speak to them. They realized that he had seen a vision in the Holy Place because he was making signs to them and remained unable to speak. When his time of service was over, he went to his home.

After some time his wife Elizabeth became pregnant, and for five months she kept herself in seclusion. She said, "This is what the Lord has done for me at the time when he has been gracious to me, to take away my disgrace among people."

BIRTH ANNOUNCEMENT OF JESUS THE MESSIAH

In the sixth month of Elizabeth's pregnancy, the angel Gabriel was sent by God to a town of Galilee called Nazareth, to a virgin engaged to a man whose name was Joseph, a descendant of David, and the virgin's name was Mary. The angel came to her and said, "Greetings, favored one, the Lord is with you!" But she was greatly troubled by his words and began to wonder about the meaning of this greeting. So the angel said to her, "Do not be afraid, Mary, for you have found favor with God! Listen: You will become pregnant and give birth to a son, and you will name him Jesus. He will be great and will be called the Son of the Most High, and the Lord God will give him the throne of his father David. He will reign over the house of Jacob forever, and his kingdom will never end." Mary said to the angel, "How will this be, since I have not been intimate with a man?" The angel replied, "The Holy Spirit will come upon you, and the power of the Most High will overshadow you. Therefore the child to be born will be holy; he will be called the Son of God.

"And look, your relative Elizabeth has also become pregnant with a son in her old age—although she was called barren, she is now in her sixth month! For nothing will be impossible with God." So Mary said, "Yes, I am a servant of the Lord; let this happen to me according to your word." Then the angel departed from her.

MARY AND ELIZABETH

In those days Mary got up and went hurriedly into the hill country, to a town of Judah, and entered Zechariah's house and greeted Elizabeth. When Elizabeth heard Mary's greeting, the baby leaped in her womb, and Elizabeth was filled with the Holy Spirit. She exclaimed with a loud voice, "Blessed are you among women, and blessed is the child in your womb! And who am I that the mother of my Lord should come and visit me? For the instant the sound of your greeting reached my ears, the baby in my womb leaped for joy. And blessed is she who believed that what was spoken to her by the Lord would be fulfilled."

MARY'S HYMN OF PRAISE

And Mary said,

"My soul exalts the Lord,
and my spirit has begun to rejoice in God my Savior,
because he has looked upon the humble state of his servant.
For from now on all generations will call me blessed,
because he who is mighty has done great things for me, and holy is his name;
from generation to generation he is merciful to those who fear him.
He has demonstrated power with his arm; he has scattered those whose pride wells up from the sheer arrogance of their hearts.
He has brought down the mighty from their thrones, and has lifted up those of lowly position;
he has filled the hungry with good things, and has sent the rich away empty.
He has helped his servant Israel, remembering his mercy,
as he promised to our ancestors, to Abraham and to his descendants forever."

So Mary stayed with Elizabeth about three months and then returned to her home.

THE BIRTH OF JOHN

Now the time came for Elizabeth to have her baby, and she gave birth to a son. Her neighbors and relatives heard that the Lord had shown great mercy to her, and they rejoiced with her.

On the eighth day they came to circumcise the child, and they wanted to name him Zechariah after his father. But his mother replied, "No! He must be named John." They said to her, "But none of your relatives bears this name." So they made signs to the baby's father, inquiring what he wanted to name his son. He asked for a writing tablet and wrote, "His name is John." And they were all amazed. Immediately Zechariah's mouth was opened and his tongue released, and he spoke, blessing God. All their neighbors were filled with fear, and throughout the entire hill country of Judea all these things were talked about. All who heard these things kept them in their hearts, saying, "What then will this child be?" For the Lord's hand was indeed with him.

ZECHARIAH'S PRAISE AND PREDICTION

Then his father Zechariah was filled with the Holy Spirit and prophesied,

"Blessed be the Lord God of Israel,
    because he has come to help and has
        redeemed his people.
For he has raised up a horn of salvation
    for us in the house of his servant David,
as he spoke through the mouth of his
    holy prophets from long ago,
that we should be saved from our enemies
    and from the hand of all who hate us.

He has done this to show mercy to our
  ancestors,
and to remember his holy covenant—
the oath that he swore to our ancestor
  Abraham.
This oath grants
that we, being rescued from the hand of
  our enemies,
may serve him without fear,
in holiness and righteousness before
  him for as long as we live.
And you, child, will be called the prophet
  of the Most High.
For you will go before the Lord to
  prepare his ways,
to give his people knowledge of salvation
  through the forgiveness of their sins.
Because of our God's tender mercy,
the dawn will break upon us from on high
to give light to those who sit in darkness
  and in the shadow of death,
to guide our feet into the way of peace."

And the child kept growing and becoming
strong in spirit, and he was in the wilderness
until the day he was revealed to Israel.

CHAPTER 2

THE CENSUS AND THE BIRTH OF JESUS
Now in those days a decree went out from
Caesar Augustus to register all the empire for
taxes. This was the first registration, taken when

Quirinius was governor of Syria. Everyone went to his own town to be registered. So Joseph also went up from the town of Nazareth in Galilee to Judea, to the city of David called Bethlehem, because he was of the house and family line of David. He went to be registered with Mary, who was promised in marriage to him, and who was expecting a child. While they were there, the time came for her to deliver her child. And she gave birth to her firstborn son and wrapped him in strips of cloth and laid him in a manger, because there was no place for them in the inn.

THE SHEPHERDS' VISIT

Now there were shepherds nearby living out in the field, keeping guard over their flock at night. An angel of the Lord appeared to them, and the glory of the Lord shone around them, and they were absolutely terrified. But the angel said to them, "Do not be afraid! Listen carefully, for I proclaim to you good news that brings great joy to all the people: Today your Savior is born in the city of David. He is Christ the Lord. This will be a sign for you: You will find a baby wrapped in strips of cloth and lying in a manger." Suddenly a vast, heavenly army appeared with the angel, praising God and saying,

"Glory to God in the highest,
and on earth peace among people with
whom he is pleased!"

When the angels left them and went back to heaven, the shepherds said to one another, "Let us go over to Bethlehem and see this thing that has taken place, that the Lord has made known to us." So they hurried off and located Mary and Joseph, and found the baby lying in a manger. When they saw him, they related what they had been told about this child, and all who heard it were astonished at what the shepherds said. But Mary treasured up all these words, pondering in her heart what they might mean. So the shepherds returned, glorifying and praising God for all they had heard and seen; everything was just as they had been told.

At the end of eight days, when he was circumcised, he was named Jesus, the name given by the angel before he was conceived in the womb.

JESUS' PRESENTATION AT THE TEMPLE

Now when the time came for their purification according to the law of Moses, Joseph and Mary brought Jesus up to Jerusalem to present him to the Lord (just as it is written in the law of the Lord, "*Every firstborn male will be set apart to the Lord*"), and to offer a sacrifice according to what is specified in the law of the Lord, *a pair of doves or two young pigeons.*

THE PROPHECY OF SIMEON

Now there was a man in Jerusalem named Simeon who was righteous and devout, looking for the restoration of Israel, and the Holy Spirit was upon him. It had been revealed to him by the Holy Spirit that he would not die before he had seen the Lord's Christ. So

Simeon, directed by the Spirit, came into the temple courts, and when the parents brought in the child Jesus to do for him what was customary according to the law, Simeon took him in his arms and blessed God, saying,

> "Now, according to your word, Sovereign Lord, permit your servant to depart in peace.
> For my eyes have seen your salvation
> that you have prepared in the presence of all peoples:
> a light,
> for revelation to the Gentiles
> and for glory to your people Israel."

So the child's father and mother were amazed at what was said about him. Then Simeon blessed them and said to his mother Mary, "Listen carefully: This child is destined to be the cause of the falling and rising of many in Israel and to be a sign that will be rejected. Indeed, as a result of him the thoughts of many hearts will be revealed—and a sword will pierce your own soul as well!"

THE TESTIMONY OF ANNA

There was also a prophetess, Anna the daughter of Phanuel, of the tribe of Asher. She was very old, having been married to her husband for seven years until his death. She had lived as a widow since then for eighty-four years. She never left the temple, worshiping with fasting and prayer night and day. At that moment, she came up to them and began to give thanks to God and to speak about the child to all who were waiting for the redemption of Jerusalem.

So when Joseph and Mary had performed everything according to the law of the Lord, they returned to Galilee, to their own town of Nazareth. And the child grew and became strong, filled with wisdom, and the favor of God was upon him.

JESUS IN THE TEMPLE

Now Jesus' parents went to Jerusalem every year for the Feast of the Passover. When he was twelve years old, they went up according to custom. But when the feast was over, as they were returning home, the boy Jesus stayed behind in Jerusalem. His parents did not know it, but (because they assumed that he was in their group of travelers) they went a day's journey. Then they began to look for him among their relatives and acquaintances. When they did not find him, they returned to Jerusalem to look for him. After three days they found him in the temple courts, sitting among the teachers, listening to them and asking them questions. And all who heard Jesus were astonished at his understanding and his answers. When his parents saw him, they were overwhelmed. His mother said to him, "Child, why have you treated us like this? Look, your father and I have been looking for you anxiously." But he replied, "Why were you looking for me? Didn't you know that I must be in my Father's house?" Yet his parents did not understand the remark he made to them. Then he went down with them and came to Nazareth, and was obedient to them. But his mother kept all these things in her heart.

And Jesus increased in wisdom and in stature and in favor with God and with people.

CHAPTER 3

THE MINISTRY OF JOHN THE BAPTIST

In the fifteenth year of the reign of Tiberius Caesar, when Pontius Pilate was governor of Judea, and Herod was tetrarch of Galilee, and his brother Philip was tetrarch of the region of Iturea and Trachonitis, and Lysanias was tetrarch of Abilene, during the high priesthood of Annas and Caiaphas, the word of God came to John the son of Zechariah in the wilderness. He went into all the region around the Jordan River, preaching a baptism of repentance for the forgiveness of sins.

As it is written in the book of the words of the prophet Isaiah,

"The voice of one shouting in the wilderness:
'Prepare the way for the Lord,
make his paths straight.
Every valley will be filled,
and every mountain and hill will be
*   brought low,*
and the crooked will be made straight,
and the rough ways will be made smooth,
and all humanity will see the salvation
*   of God.' "*

So John said to the crowds that came out to be baptized by him, "You offspring of vipers! Who warned you to flee from the coming wrath? Therefore produce fruit that proves your repentance, and don't begin to say to yourselves, 'We have Abraham as our father.' For I tell you that God can raise up children for Abraham from these stones! Even now the ax is laid at the root of the trees, and every tree that does not produce good fruit will be cut down and thrown into the fire."

So the crowds were asking him, "What then should we do?" John answered them, "The person who has two tunics must share with the person who has none, and the person who has food must do likewise." Tax collectors also came to be baptized, and they said to him, "Teacher, what should we do?" He told them, "Collect no more than you are required to." Then some soldiers also asked him, "And as for us—what should we do?" He told them, "Take money from no one by violence or by false accusation, and be content with your pay."

While the people were filled with anticipation and they all wondered whether perhaps John could be the Christ, John answered them all, "I baptize you with water, but one more powerful than I am is coming—I am not worthy to untie the strap of his sandals. He will baptize you with the Holy Spirit and fire. His winnowing fork is in his hand to clean out his threshing floor and to gather the wheat into his storehouse, but the chaff he will burn up with inextinguishable fire."

And in this way, with many other exhortations, John proclaimed good news to the people. But when John rebuked Herod the tetrarch because of Herodias, his brother's wife, and because of all the evil deeds that he had done, Herod added this to them all: He locked up John in prison.

THE BAPTISM OF JESUS
Now when all the people were baptized, Jesus also was baptized. And while he was praying, the heavens opened, and the Holy Spirit descended on him in bodily form like a dove. And a voice came from heaven, "You are my one dear Son; in you I take great delight."

THE GENEALOGY OF JESUS
So Jesus, when he began his ministry, was about thirty years old. He was the son (as was supposed) of Joseph, the son of Heli, the son of Matthat, the son of Levi, the son of Melchi, the son of Jannai, the son of Joseph, the son of Mattathias, the son of Amos, the son of Nahum, the son of Esli, the son of Naggai, the son of Maath, the son of Mattathias, the son of Semein, the son of Josech, the son of Joda, the son of Joanan, the son of Rhesa, the son of Zerubbabel, the son of Shealtiel, the son of Neri, the son of Melchi, the son of Addi, the son of Cosam, the son of Elmadam, the son of Er, the son of Joshua, the son of Eliezer, the son of Jorim, the son of Matthat, the son of Levi, the son of Simeon, the son of Judah, the son of

Joseph, the son of Jonam, the son of Eliakim, the son of Melea, the son of Menna, the son of Mattatha, the son of Nathan, the son of David, the son of Jesse, the son of Obed, the son of Boaz, the son of Sala, the son of Nahshon, the son of Amminadab, the son of Admin, the son of Arni, the son of Hezron, the son of Perez, the son of Judah, the son of Jacob, the son of Isaac, the son of Abraham, the son of Terah, the son of Nahor, the son of Serug, the son of Reu, the son of Peleg, the son of Eber, the son of Shelah, the son of Cainan, the son of Arphaxad, the son of Shem, the son of Noah, the son of Lamech, the son of Methuselah, the son of Enoch, the son of Jared, the son of Mahalalel, the son of Kenan, the son of Enosh, the son of Seth, the son of Adam, the son of God.

CHAPTER 4

THE TEMPTATION OF JESUS

Then Jesus, full of the Holy Spirit, returned from the Jordan River and was led by the Spirit in the wilderness, where for forty days he endured temptations from the devil. He ate nothing during those days, and when they were completed, he was famished. The devil said to him, "If you are the Son of God, command this stone to become bread." Jesus answered him, "It is written, *'Man does not live by bread alone.'*"

Then the devil led him up to a high place and showed him in a flash all the kingdoms of the world. And he said to him, "To you I will grant this whole realm—and the glory that goes along with it, for it has been relinquished to me, and I can give it to anyone I wish. So then, if you will worship me, all this will be yours." Jesus answered him, "It is written, '*You are to worship the Lord your God and serve* only *him.*'"

Then the devil brought him to Jerusalem, had him stand on the highest point of the temple, and said to him, "If you are the Son of God, throw yourself down from here, for it is written, '*He will command his angels concerning you, to protect you,*' and '*with their hands they will lift you up, so that you will not strike your foot against a stone.*'" Jesus answered him, "It is said, '*You are not to put the Lord your God to the test.*'" So when the devil had completed every temptation, he departed from him until a more opportune time.

THE BEGINNING OF JESUS' MINISTRY IN GALILEE

Then Jesus, in the power of the Spirit, returned to Galilee, and news about him spread throughout the surrounding countryside. He began to teach in their synagogues and was praised by all.

REJECTION AT NAZARETH

Now Jesus came to Nazareth, where he had been brought up, and went into the synagogue on the Sabbath day, as was his custom. He stood up to read, and the scroll of the prophet Isaiah was given to him. He unrolled the scroll and found the place where it was written,

> "The Spirit of the Lord is upon me,
> because he has anointed me to proclaim
>   good news to the poor.
> He has sent me to proclaim release to the
>   captives
> and the regaining of sight to the blind,
> to set free those who are oppressed,
> to proclaim the year of the Lord's favor."

Then he rolled up the scroll, gave it back to the attendant, and sat down. The eyes of everyone in the synagogue were fixed on him. Then he began to tell them, "Today this scripture has been fulfilled even as you heard it being read." All were speaking well of him, and were amazed at the gracious words coming out of his mouth. They said, "Isn't this Joseph's son?" Jesus said to them, "No doubt you will quote to me the proverb, 'Physician, heal yourself!' and say, 'What we have heard that you did in Capernaum, do here in your hometown too.'" And he added, "I tell you the truth, no prophet is acceptable in his hometown. But in truth I tell you, there were many widows in Israel in Elijah's days, when the sky was shut up three and a half years and there was a great famine over all the land. Yet Elijah was sent to none of them, but only to a woman who was a widow at Zarephath in Sidon. And there were many lepers in Israel in the time of the prophet Elisha, yet none of them was cleansed except

Naaman the Syrian." When they heard this, all the people in the synagogue were filled with rage. They got up, forced him out of the town, and brought him to the brow of the hill on which their town was built, so that they could throw him down the cliff. But he passed through the crowd and went on his way.

MINISTRY IN CAPERNAUM

So he went down to Capernaum, a town in Galilee, and on the Sabbath he began to teach the people. They were amazed at his teaching because he spoke with authority.

Now in the synagogue there was a man who had the spirit of an unclean demon, and he cried out with a loud voice, "Ha! Leave us alone, Jesus the Nazarene! Have you come to destroy us? I know who you are—the Holy One of God." But Jesus rebuked him: "Silence! Come out of him!" Then, after the demon threw the man down in their midst, he came out of him without hurting him. They were all amazed and began to say to one another, "What's happening here? For with authority and power he commands the unclean spirits, and they come out!" So the news about him spread into all areas of the region.

After Jesus left the synagogue, he entered Simon's house. Now Simon's mother-in-law was suffering from a high fever, and they asked Jesus to help her. So he stood over her, commanded the fever, and it left her. Immediately she got up and began to serve them.

As the sun was setting, all those who had any relatives sick with various diseases brought them to Jesus. He placed his hands on every one of them and healed them. Demons also came out of many, crying out, "You are the Son of God!" But he rebuked them and would not allow them to speak because they knew that he was the Christ.

The next morning Jesus departed and went to a deserted place. Yet the crowds were seeking him, and they came to him and tried to keep him from leaving them. But Jesus said to them, "I must proclaim the good news of the kingdom of God to the other towns too, for that is what I was sent to do." So he continued to preach in the synagogues of Judea.

CHAPTER 5

THE CALL OF THE DISCIPLES

Now Jesus was standing by the Lake of Gennesaret, and the crowd was pressing around him to hear the word of God. He saw two boats by the lake, but the fishermen had gotten out of them and were washing their nets. He got into one of the boats, which was Simon's, and asked him to put out a little way from the shore. Then Jesus sat down and taught the crowds from the boat. When he had finished speaking, he said to Simon, "Put out into the deep water and lower your nets for a catch." Simon answered, "Master, we worked hard all night and caught nothing! But at your word I will lower the nets."

When they had done this, they caught so many fish that their nets started to tear. So they motioned to their partners in the other boat to come and help them. And they came and filled both boats, so that they were about to sink. But when Simon Peter saw it, he fell down at Jesus' knees, saying, "Go away from me, Lord, for I am a sinful man!" For Peter and all who were with him were astonished at the catch of fish that they had taken, and so were James and John, Zebedee's sons, who were Simon's business partners. Then Jesus said to Simon, "Do not be afraid; from now on you will be catching people!" So when they had brought their boats to shore, they left everything and followed him.

HEALING A LEPER

While Jesus was in one of the towns, a man came to him who was covered with leprosy. When he saw Jesus, he bowed down with his face to the ground and begged him, "Lord, if you are willing, you can make me clean." So he stretched out his hand and touched him, saying, "I am willing. Be clean!" And immediately the leprosy left him. Then he ordered the man to tell no one, but commanded him, "Go and show yourself to a priest, and bring the offering for your cleansing, as Moses commanded, as a testimony to them." But the news about him spread even more, and large crowds were gathering together to hear him and to be healed of their illnesses. Yet Jesus himself frequently withdrew to the wilderness and prayed.

HEALING AND FORGIVING A PARALYTIC

Now on one of those days, while he was teaching, there were Pharisees and teachers of the law sitting nearby (who had come from every village of Galilee and Judea and from Jerusalem), and the power of the Lord was with him to heal. Just then some men showed up, carrying a paralyzed man on a stretcher. They were trying to bring him in and place him before Jesus. But since they found no way to carry him in because of the crowd, they went up on the roof and let him down on the stretcher through the roof tiles right in front of Jesus. When Jesus saw their faith, he said, "Friend, your sins are forgiven." Then the experts in the law and the Pharisees began to think to themselves, "Who is this man who is uttering blasphemies? Who can forgive sins but God alone?" When Jesus perceived their hostile thoughts, he said to them, "Why are you raising objections within yourselves? Which is easier, to say, 'Your sins are forgiven,' or to say, 'Stand up and walk'? But so that you may know that the Son of Man has authority on earth to forgive sins"—he said to the paralyzed man—"I tell you, stand up, take your stretcher and go home." Immediately he stood up before them, picked up the stretcher he had been lying on, and went home, glorifying God. Then astonishment seized them all, and they glorified God. They were filled with awe, saying, "We have seen incredible things today."

THE CALL OF LEVI; EATING WITH SINNERS

After this, Jesus went out and saw a tax collector named Levi sitting at the tax booth. "Follow me," he said to him. And he got up and followed him, leaving everything behind.

Then Levi gave a great banquet in his house for Jesus, and there was a large crowd of tax collectors and others sitting at the table with them. But the Pharisees and their experts in the law complained to his disciples, saying, "Why do you eat and drink with tax collectors and sinners?" Jesus answered them, "Those who are well don't need a physician, but those who are sick do. I have not come to call the righteous, but sinners to repentance."

THE SUPERIORITY OF THE NEW

Then they said to him, "John's disciples frequently fast and pray, and so do the disciples of the Pharisees, but yours continue to eat and drink." So Jesus said to them, "You cannot make the wedding guests fast while the bridegroom is with them, can you? But those days are coming, and when the bridegroom is taken from them, at that time they will fast." He also told them a parable: "No one tears a patch from a new garment and sews it on an old garment. If he does, he will have torn the new, and the piece from the new will not match the old. And no one pours new wine into old wineskins. If he does, the new wine will burst the skins and will be spilled, and the skins will be destroyed. Instead new wine must be poured into new wineskins. No one after drinking old wine wants the new, for he says, 'The old is good enough.'"

CHAPTER 6

LORD OF THE SABBATH

Jesus was going through the grain fields on a Sabbath, and his disciples picked some heads of wheat, rubbed them in their hands, and ate them. But some of the Pharisees said, "Why are you doing what is against the law on the Sabbath?" Jesus answered them, "Haven't you read what David did when he and his companions were hungry—how he entered the house of God, took and ate the sacred bread, which is not lawful for any to eat but the priests alone, and gave it to his companions?" Then he said to them, "The Son of Man is lord of the Sabbath."

HEALING A WITHERED HAND

On another Sabbath, Jesus entered the synagogue and was teaching. Now a man was there whose right hand was withered. The experts in the law and the Pharisees watched Jesus closely to see if he would heal on the Sabbath, so that they could find a reason to accuse him. But he knew their thoughts, and said to the man who had the withered hand, "Get up and stand here." So he rose and stood there. Then Jesus said to them, "I ask you, is it lawful to do good on the Sabbath or to do evil, to save a life or to destroy it?" After looking around at them all, he said to the man, "Stretch out your hand." The man did so, and his hand was restored. But they were filled with mindless rage and began debating with one another what they would do to Jesus.

CHOOSING THE 12 APOSTLES

Now it was during this time that Jesus went out to the mountain to pray, and he spent all night in prayer to God. When morning came, he called his disciples and chose 12 of them, whom he also named apostles: Simon (whom he named Peter), and his brother Andrew; and James, John, Philip, Bartholomew, Matthew, Thomas, James the son of Alphaeus, Simon who was called the Zealot, Judas the son of James, and Judas Iscariot, who became a traitor.

THE SERMON ON THE PLAIN

Then he came down with them and stood on a level place. And a large number of his disciples had gathered along with a vast multitude from all over Judea, from Jerusalem, and from the seacoast of Tyre and Sidon. They came to hear him and to be healed of their diseases, and those who suffered from unclean spirits were cured. The whole crowd was trying to touch him because power was coming out from him and healing them all.

Then he looked up at his disciples and said:

"Blessed are you who are poor, for the kingdom of God belongs to you.

"Blessed are you who hunger now, for you will be satisfied.

"Blessed are you who weep now, for you will laugh.

"Blessed are you when people hate you, and when they exclude you and insult you and reject you as evil on account of the Son of Man! Rejoice in that day, and jump for joy because your reward is great in heaven. For their ancestors did the same things to the prophets.

"But woe to you who are rich, for you have received your comfort already.

"Woe to you who are well satisfied with food now, for you will be hungry.

"Woe to you who laugh now, for you will mourn and weep.

"Woe to you when all people speak well of you, for their ancestors did the same things to the false prophets.

"But I say to you who are listening: Love your enemies, do good to those who hate you, bless those who curse you, pray for those who mistreat you. To the person who strikes you on the cheek, offer the other as well, and from the person who takes away your coat, do not withhold your tunic either. Give to everyone who asks you, and do not ask for your possessions back from the person who takes them away. Treat others in the same way that you would want them to treat you.

"If you love those who love you, what credit is that to you? For even sinners love those who love them. And if you do good to those who do good to you, what credit is that to you? Even sinners do the same. And if you lend to those from whom you hope to be repaid, what credit is that to you? Even sinners lend to sinners, so that they may be repaid in full. But love your enemies, and do good, and lend, expecting nothing back. Then your reward will be great, and you will be sons of the Most High, because he is kind to ungrateful and evil people. Be merciful, just as your Father is merciful.

DO NOT JUDGE OTHERS

"Do not judge, and you will not be judged; do not condemn, and you will not be condemned; forgive, and you will be forgiven. Give, and it will be given to you: A good measure, pressed down, shaken together, running over, will be poured into your lap. For the measure you use will be the measure you receive."

He also told them a parable: "Someone who is blind cannot lead another who is blind, can he? Won't they both fall into a pit? A disciple is not greater than his teacher, but everyone when fully trained will be like his teacher. Why do you see the speck in your brother's eye, but fail to see the beam of wood in your own? How can you say to your brother, 'Brother, let me remove the speck from your eye,' while you yourself don't see the beam in your own? You hypocrite! First remove the beam from your own eye, and then you can see clearly to re-move the speck from your brother's eye.

"For no good tree bears bad fruit, nor again does a bad tree bear good fruit, for each tree is known by its own fruit. For figs are not gathered from thorns, nor are grapes picked from bram-bles. The good person out of the good treasury of his heart produces good, and the evil person out of his evil treasury produces evil, for his mouth speaks from what fills his heart.

"Why do you call me 'Lord, Lord,' and don't do what I tell you?

"Everyone who comes to me and listens to my words and puts them into practice—I will show you what he is like: He is like a man building a house, who dug down deep and laid the foundation on bedrock. When a flood came, the river burst against that house but could not shake it because it had been well built. But the person who hears and does not put my words into practice is like a man who built a house on the ground without a foundation. When the river burst against that house, it collapsed immediately and was utterly destroyed!"

CHAPTER 7

HEALING THE CENTURION'S SLAVE

After Jesus had finished teaching all this to the people, he entered Capernaum. A centurion there had a slave who was highly regarded, but who was sick and at the point of death. When the centurion heard about Jesus, he sent some Jewish elders to him, asking him to come and heal his slave. When they came to Jesus, they urged him earnestly, "He is worthy to have you do this for him because he loves our nation and even built our synagogue." So Jesus went with them. When he was not far from the house, the centurion sent friends to say to him, "Lord, do not trouble yourself, for

I am not worthy to have you come under my roof! That is why I did not presume to come to you. Instead, say the word, and my servant must be healed. For I too am a man set under authority, with soldiers under me. I say to this one, 'Go!' and he goes, and to another, 'Come!' and he comes, and to my slave, 'Do this!' and he does it." When Jesus heard this, he was amazed at him. He turned and said to the crowd that followed him, "I tell you, not even in Israel have I found such faith!" So when those who had been sent returned to the house, they found the slave well.

RAISING A WIDOW'S SON

Soon afterward Jesus went to a town called Nain, and his disciples and a large crowd went with him. As he approached the town gate, a man who had died was being carried out, the only son of his mother (who was a widow), and a large crowd from the town was with her. When the Lord saw her, he had compassion for her and said to her, "Do not weep." Then he came up and touched the bier, and those who carried it stood still. He said, "Young man, I say to you, get up!" So the dead man sat up and began to speak, and Jesus gave him back to his mother. Fear seized them all, and they began to glorify God, saying, "A great prophet has appeared among us!" and "God has come to help his people!" This report about Jesus circulated throughout Judea and all the surrounding country.

JESUS AND JOHN THE BAPTIST

John's disciples informed him about all these things. So John called two of his disciples and sent them to Jesus to ask, "Are you the one who is to come, or should we look for another?" When the men came to Jesus, they said, "John the Baptist has sent us to you to ask, 'Are you the one who is to come, or should we look for another?' " At that very time Jesus cured many people of diseases, sicknesses, and evil spirits, and granted sight to many who were blind. So he answered them, "Go tell John what you have seen and heard: The blind see, the lame walk, lepers are cleansed, the deaf hear, the dead are raised, the poor have good news proclaimed to them. Blessed is anyone who takes no offense at me."

When John's messengers had gone, Jesus began to speak to the crowds about John: "What did you go out into the wilderness to see? A reed shaken by the wind? What did you go out to see? A man dressed in soft clothing? Look, those who wear soft clothing and live in luxury are in the royal palaces! What did you go out to see? A prophet? Yes, I tell you, and more than a prophet. This is the one about whom it is written, '*Look, I am sending my messenger ahead of you, who will prepare your way before you.*' I tell you, among those born of women no one is greater than John. Yet the one who is least in the kingdom of God is greater than he is." (Now all the people who heard this, even the tax collectors, acknowledged God's justice because they had been baptized with John's baptism. However, the Pharisees and the experts in religious law rejected God's purpose for themselves because they had not been baptized by John.)

"To what then should I compare the people of this generation, and what are they like? They are like children sitting in the marketplace and calling out to one another,

" 'We played the flute for you, yet you did not dance;
we wailed in mourning, yet you did not weep.'

For John the Baptist has come eating no bread and drinking no wine, and you say, 'He has a demon!' The Son of Man has come eating and drinking, and you say, 'Look at him, a glutton and a drunk, a friend of tax collectors and sinners!' But wisdom is vindicated by all her children."

JESUS' ANOINTING

Now one of the Pharisees asked Jesus to have dinner with him, so he went into the Pharisee's house and took his place at the table. Then when a woman of that town, who was a sinner, learned that Jesus was dining at the Pharisee's house, she brought an alabaster jar of perfumed oil. As she stood behind him at his feet, weeping, she began to wet his feet with her tears. She wiped them with her hair, kissed them, and anointed them with the perfumed oil. Now when the Pharisee who had invited him saw this, he said to himself, "If this man were a prophet, he would know who and what kind of woman this is who is touching him, that she is a sinner." So Jesus answered him, "Simon, I have something to say to you." He replied, "Say it, Teacher." "A certain creditor had two debtors; one owed him 500 silver coins, and the other 50. When they could not pay, he canceled the debts of both. Now which of them will love him more?" Simon answered, "I suppose the one who had the bigger debt canceled." Jesus said to him, "You have judged rightly." Then, turning toward the woman, he said to Simon, "Do you see this woman? I entered your house. You gave me no water for my feet, but she has wet my feet with her tears and wiped them with her hair. You gave me no kiss of greeting, but from the time I entered she has not stopped kissing my feet. You did not anoint my head with oil, but she has anointed my feet with perfumed oil. Therefore I tell you, her sins, which were many, are forgiven, thus she loved much; but the one who is forgiven little loves little." Then Jesus said to her, "Your sins are forgiven." But those who were at the table with him began to say among themselves, "Who is this, who even forgives sins?" He said to the woman, "Your faith has saved you; go in peace."

CHAPTER 8

JESUS' MINISTRY AND THE HELP OF WOMEN

Sometime afterward he went on through towns and villages, preaching and proclaiming the good news of the kingdom of God. The twelve were with him, and also some women who had been healed of evil spirits and disabilities: Mary (called Magdalene), from whom seven demons had gone out, and Joanna the wife of Cuza (Herod's household manager), Susanna, and many others who provided for them out of their own resources.

THE PARABLE OF THE SOWER

While a large crowd was gathering and people were coming to Jesus from one town after another, he spoke to them in a parable: "A sower went out to sow his seed. And as he sowed, some fell along the path and was trampled on, and the wild birds devoured it. Other seed fell on rock, and when it came up, it withered because it had no moisture. Other seed fell among the thorns, and they grew up with it and choked it. But other seed fell on good soil and grew, and it produced a hundred times as much grain." As he said this, he called out, "The one who has ears to hear had better listen!"

Then his disciples asked him what this parable meant. He said, "You have been given the opportunity to know the secrets of the kingdom of God, but for others they are in parables, so that *although they see they may not see, and although they hear they may not understand.*

"Now the parable means this: The seed is the word of God. Those along the path are the ones who have heard; then the devil comes and takes away the word from their hearts, so that they may not believe and be saved. Those on the rock are the ones who receive the word with joy when they hear it, but they have no root. They believe for a while, but in a time of testing fall away. As for the seed that fell among thorns, these are the ones who hear, but as they go on their way they are choked by the worries and riches and pleasures of life, and their fruit does not mature. But as for the seed that landed on good soil, these are the ones who, after hearing the word, cling to it with an honest and good heart, and bear fruit with steadfast endurance.

SHOWING THE LIGHT

"No one lights a lamp and then covers it with a jar or puts it under a bed, but puts it on a lampstand so that those who come in can see the light. For nothing is hidden that will not be revealed, and nothing concealed that will not be made known and brought to light. So listen carefully, for whoever has will be given more, but whoever does not have, even what he thinks he has will be taken from him."

JESUS' TRUE FAMILY

Now Jesus' mother and his brothers came to him, but they could not get near him because of the crowd. So he was told, "Your mother and your brothers are standing outside, wanting to see you." But he replied to them, "My mother and my brothers are those who hear the word of God and do it."

STILLING OF A STORM

One day Jesus got into a boat with his disciples and said to them, "Let's go across to the other side of the lake." So they set out, and as they sailed he fell asleep. Now a violent windstorm came down on the lake, and the boat started filling up with water, and they were in danger. They came and woke him, saying, "Master, Master, we are about to die!" So he got up and rebuked the wind and the raging waves; they died down, and it was calm. Then he said to them, "Where is your faith?" But they were afraid and amazed, saying to one another, "Who then is this? He commands even the winds and the water, and they obey him!"

HEALING OF A DEMONIAC

So they sailed over to the region of the Gerasenes, which is opposite Galilee. As Jesus stepped ashore, a certain man from the town met him who was possessed by demons. For a long time this man had worn no clothes and had not lived in a house, but among the tombs. When he saw Jesus, he cried out, fell down before him, and shouted with a loud voice, "Leave me alone, Jesus, Son of the Most High God! I beg you, do not torment me!" For Jesus had started commanding the evil spirit to come out of the man. (For it had seized him many times, so he would be bound with chains and shackles and kept under guard. But he would break the restraints and be driven by the demon into deserted places.) Jesus then asked him, "What is your name?" He said, "Legion," because many demons had entered him. And they began to beg him not to order them to depart into the abyss. Now a large herd of pigs was feeding there on the hillside, and the demonic spirits begged Jesus to let them go into them. He gave them permission. So the demons came out of the man and went into the pigs, and the herd of pigs rushed down the steep slope into the lake and drowned. When the herdsmen saw what had happened, they ran off and spread the news in the town and countryside. So the people went out to see what had happened, and they came to Jesus. They found the man from whom the demons had gone out, sitting at Jesus' feet, clothed and in his right mind, and they were afraid. Those who had seen it told them how the man who had been demon-possessed had been healed. Then all the people of the Gerasenes and the surrounding region asked Jesus to leave them alone, for they were seized with great fear. So he got into the boat and left. The man from whom the demons had gone out begged to go with him, but Jesus sent him away, saying, "Return to your home, and declare what God has done for you." So he went away, proclaiming throughout the whole town what Jesus had done for him.

RESTORATION AND HEALING

Now when Jesus returned, the crowd welcomed him because they were all waiting for him. Then a man named Jairus, who was a leader of the synagogue, came up. Falling at Jesus' feet, he pleaded with him to come to his house, because he had an only daughter, about twelve years old, and she was dying.

As Jesus was on his way, the crowds pressed around him. Now a woman was there who had been suffering from a hemorrhage for twelve years but could not be healed by anyone. She came up behind Jesus and touched the edge of his cloak, and at once the bleeding stopped. Then Jesus asked, "Who was it who touched me?" When they all denied it, Peter said, "Master, the crowds are surrounding you and pressing against you!" But Jesus said, "Someone touched me, for I know that power has gone out from me." When the woman saw that she could not escape notice, she came trembling and fell down before him. In the presence of all the people, she explained why she had touched him and how she had been immediately healed. Then he said to her, "Daughter, your faith has made you well. Go in peace."

While he was still speaking, someone from the synagogue leader's house came and said, "Your daughter is dead; do not trouble the teacher any longer." But when Jesus heard this, he told him, "Do not be afraid; just believe, and she will be healed." Now when he came to the house, Jesus did not let anyone go in with him except Peter, John, and James, and the child's father and mother. Now they were all wailing and mourning for her, but he said, "Stop your weeping; she is not dead but asleep!" And they began making fun of him because they knew that she was dead. But Jesus gently took her by the hand and said, "Child, get up." Her spirit returned, and she got up immediately. Then he told them to give her something to eat. Her parents were astonished, but he ordered them to tell no one what had happened.

CHAPTER 9

THE SENDING OF THE 12 APOSTLES

After Jesus called the twelve together, he gave them power and authority over all demons and to cure diseases, and he sent them out to proclaim the kingdom of God and to heal the sick. He said to them, "Take nothing for your journey—no staff, no bag, no bread, no money, and do not take an extra tunic. Whatever house you enter, stay there until you leave the area.

Wherever they do not receive you, as you leave that town, shake the dust off your feet as a testimony against them." Then they departed and went throughout the villages, proclaiming the good news and healing people everywhere.

HEROD'S CONFUSION ABOUT JESUS

Now Herod the tetrarch heard about everything that was happening, and he was thoroughly perplexed because some people were saying that John had been raised from the dead, while others were saying that Elijah had appeared, and still others that one of the prophets of long ago had risen. Herod said, "I had John beheaded, but who is this about whom I hear such things?" So Herod wanted to learn about Jesus.

THE FEEDING OF THE 5,000

When the apostles returned, they told Jesus everything they had done. Then he took them with him and they withdrew privately to a town called Bethsaida. But when the crowds found out, they followed him. He welcomed them, spoke to them about the kingdom of God, and cured those who needed healing. Now the day began to draw to a close, so the twelve came and said to Jesus, "Send the crowd away, so they can go into the surrounding villages and countryside and find lodging and food because we are in an isolated place." But he said to them, "You give them something to eat." They replied, "We have no more than five loaves and two fish—unless we go and buy food for all these people." (Now about 5,000 men were there.) Then he said to his disciples, "Have them sit down in groups of about fifty each." So they did as Jesus directed, and the people all sat down.

Then he took the five loaves and the two fish, and looking up to heaven he gave thanks and broke them. He gave them to the disciples to set before the crowd. They all ate and were satisfied, and what was left over was picked up—12 baskets of broken pieces.

PETER'S CONFESSION

Once when Jesus was praying by himself and his disciples were nearby, he asked them, "Who do the crowds say that I am?" They answered, "John the Baptist; others say Elijah; and still others that one of the prophets of long ago has risen." Then he said to them, "But who do you say that I am?" Peter answered, "The Christ of God." But he forcefully commanded them not to tell this to anyone, saying, "The Son of Man must suffer many things and be rejected by the elders, chief priests, and experts in the law, and be killed, and on the third day be raised."

A CALL TO DISCIPLESHIP

Then he said to them all, "If anyone wants to become my follower, he must deny himself, take up his cross daily, and follow me. For whoever wants to save his life will lose it, but whoever loses his life because of me will save it. For what does it benefit a person if he gains the whole world but loses or forfeits himself? For whoever is ashamed of me and my words, the Son of Man will be ashamed of that person when he comes in his glory and in the glory of the Father and of the holy angels. But I tell you most certainly, there are some standing here who will not experience death before they see the kingdom of God."

THE TRANSFIGURATION

Now about eight days after these sayings, Jesus took with him Peter, John, and James, and went up the mountain to pray. As he was praying, the appearance of his face was transformed, and his clothes became very bright, a brilliant white. Then two men, Moses and Elijah, began talking with him. They appeared in glorious splendor and spoke about his departure that he was about to carry out at Jerusalem. Now Peter and those with him were quite sleepy, but as they became fully awake, they saw his glory and the two men standing with him. Then as the men were starting to leave, Peter said to Jesus, "Master, it is good for us to be here. Let us make three shelters, one for you and one for Moses and one for Elijah"—not knowing what he was saying. As he was saying this, a cloud came and overshadowed them, and they were afraid as they entered the cloud. Then a voice came from the cloud, saying, "This is my Son, my Chosen One. Listen to him!" After the voice had spoken, Jesus was found alone. So they kept silent and told no one at that time anything of what they had seen.

HEALING A BOY WITH AN UNCLEAN SPIRIT

Now on the next day, when they had come down from the mountain, a large crowd met him. Then a man from the crowd cried out, "Teacher, I beg you to look at my son—he is my only child! A spirit seizes him, and he suddenly screams; it throws him into convulsions and causes him to foam at the mouth. It hardly ever leaves him alone, torturing him severely. I begged your disciples to cast it out, but they could not do so." Jesus answered, "You unbelieving and perverse generation! How much longer must I be with you and endure you? Bring your son here." As the boy was approaching, the demon threw him to the ground and shook him with convulsions. But Jesus rebuked the unclean spirit, healed the boy, and gave him back to his father. Then they were all astonished at the mighty power of God.

ANOTHER PREDICTION OF JESUS' SUFFERING

But while the entire crowd was amazed at everything Jesus was doing, he said to his disciples, "Take these words to heart, for the Son of Man is going to be betrayed into the hands of men." But they did not understand this statement; its meaning had been concealed from them, so that they could not grasp it. Yet they were afraid to ask him about this statement.

CONCERNING THE GREATEST

Now an argument started among the disciples as to which of them might be the greatest. But when Jesus discerned their innermost thoughts, he took a child, had him stand by his side, and said to them, "Whoever welcomes this child in my name welcomes me, and whoever welcomes me welcomes the one who sent me, for the one who is least among you all is the one who is great."

ON THE RIGHT SIDE

John answered, "Master, we saw someone casting out demons in your name, and we tried to stop him because he is not a disciple along with us." But Jesus said to him, "Do not stop him, for whoever is not against you is for you."

REJECTION IN SAMARIA

Now when the days drew near for him to be taken up, Jesus set out resolutely to go to Jerusalem. He sent messengers on ahead of him. As they went along, they entered a Samaritan village to make things ready in advance for him, but the villagers refused to welcome him because he was determined to go to Jerusalem. Now when his disciples James and John saw this, they said, "Lord, do you want us *to call fire to come down from heaven and consume them*?" But Jesus turned and rebuked them, and they went on to another village.

CHALLENGING PROFESSED FOLLOWERS

As they were walking along the road, someone said to him, "I will follow you wherever you go." Jesus said to him, "Foxes have dens and the birds in the sky have nests, but the Son of Man has no place to lay his head." Jesus said to another, "Follow me." But he replied, "Lord, first let me go and bury my father." But Jesus said to him, "Let the dead bury their own dead, but as for you, go and proclaim the kingdom of God." Yet another said, "I will follow you, Lord, but first let me say goodbye to my family." Jesus said to him, "No one who puts his hand to the plow and looks back is fit for the kingdom of God."

CHAPTER 10

THE MISSION OF THE SEVENTY-TWO

After this the Lord appointed seventy-two others and sent them on ahead of him two by two into every town and place where he himself was about to go. He said to them, "The harvest is plentiful, but the workers are few. Therefore ask the Lord of the harvest to send out workers into his harvest. Go! I am sending you out like lambs surrounded by wolves. Do not carry a money bag, a traveler's bag, or sandals, and greet no one on the road. Whenever you enter a house, first say, 'May peace be on this house!' And if a peace-loving person is there, your peace will remain on him, but if not, it will return to you. Stay in that same house, eating and drinking what they give you, for the worker deserves his pay. Do not move around from house to house. Whenever you enter a town and the people welcome you, eat what is set before you. Heal the sick in that town and say to them, 'The kingdom of God has come upon you!' But whenever you enter a town and the people do not welcome you, go into its streets and say, 'Even the dust of your town that clings to our feet we wipe off against you. Nevertheless know this: The kingdom of God has come.' I tell you, it will be more bearable on that day for Sodom than for that town!

"Woe to you, Chorazin! Woe to you, Bethsaida! For if the miracles done in you had been done in Tyre and Sidon, they would have repented long ago, sitting in sackcloth and ashes. But it will be more bearable for Tyre and Sidon in the judgment than for you! And you, Capernaum, will you be exalted to heaven? No, you will be thrown down to Hades!

"The one who listens to you listens to me, and the one who rejects you rejects me, and the one who rejects me rejects the one who sent me."

Then the seventy-two returned with joy, saying, "Lord, even the demons submit to us in your name!" So he said to them, "I saw Satan fall like lightning from heaven. Look, I have given you authority to tread on snakes and scorpions and on the full force of the enemy, and nothing will hurt you. Nevertheless, do not rejoice that the spirits submit to you, but rejoice that your names stand written in heaven."

On that same occasion Jesus rejoiced in the Holy Spirit and said, "I praise you, Father, Lord of heaven and earth, because you have hidden these things from the wise and intelligent and revealed them to little children. Yes, Father, for this was your gracious will. All things have been given to me by my Father. No one knows who the Son is except the Father, or who the Father is except the Son and anyone to whom the Son decides to reveal him."

Then Jesus turned to his disciples and said privately, "Blessed are the eyes that see what you see! For I tell you that many prophets and kings longed to see what you see but did not see it, and to hear what you hear but did not hear it."

THE PARABLE OF THE GOOD SAMARITAN

Now an expert in religious law stood up to test Jesus, saying, "Teacher, what must I do to inherit eternal life?" He said to him, "What is written in the law? How do you understand it?" The expert answered, "*Love the Lord your God with all your heart, with all your soul, with all your strength, and with all your mind,* and *love your neighbor as yourself.*" Jesus said to him, "You have answered correctly; do this, and you will live."

But the expert, wanting to justify himself, said to Jesus, "And who is my neighbor?" Jesus replied, "A man was going down from Jerusalem to Jericho, and fell into the hands of robbers, who stripped him, beat him up, and went off, leaving him half dead. Now by chance a priest was going down that road, but when he saw the injured man, he passed by on the other side. So too a Levite, when he came up to the place and saw him, passed by on the other side. But a Samaritan who was traveling came to where the injured man was, and when he saw him, he felt compassion for him. He went up to him and bandaged his wounds, pouring olive oil and wine on them. Then he put him on his own animal, brought him to an inn, and took care of him. The next day he took out two silver coins and gave them to the innkeeper, saying, 'Take care of him, and whatever else you spend, I will repay you when I come back this way.' Which of these three do you think became a neighbor to the man who fell into the hands of the robbers?" The expert in religious law said, "The one who showed mercy to him." So Jesus said to him, "Go and do the same."

JESUS AND MARTHA

Now as they went on their way, Jesus entered a certain village where a woman named Martha welcomed him as a guest. She had a sister named Mary, who sat at the Lord's feet and listened to what he said. But Martha was distracted with all the preparations she had to make, so she came up to him and said, "Lord, don't you care that my sister has left me to do all the work alone? Tell her to help me." But the Lord answered her, "Martha, Martha, you are worried and troubled about many things, but one thing is needed. Mary has chosen the best part; it will not be taken away from her."

CHAPTER 11

INSTRUCTIONS ON PRAYER

Now Jesus was praying in a certain place. When he stopped, one of his disciples said to him, "Lord, teach us to pray, just as John taught his disciples." So he said to them, "When you pray, say:

" 'Father, may your name be honored;
may your kingdom come.
Give us each day our daily bread,
and forgive us our sins,
for we also forgive everyone who sins
against us.
And do not lead us into temptation.' "

Then he said to them, "Suppose one of you has a friend, and you go to him at midnight and say to him, 'Friend, lend me three loaves of bread, because a friend of mine has stopped here while on a journey, and I have nothing to set before him.' Then he will reply from inside, 'Do not bother me. The door is already shut, and my children and I are in bed. I cannot get up and give you anything.' I tell you, even though the man inside will not get up and give him anything because he is his friend, yet because of the first man's sheer persistence he will get up and give him whatever he needs.

"So I tell you: Ask, and it will be given to you; seek, and you will find; knock, and the door will be opened for you. For everyone who asks receives, and the one who seeks finds, and to the one who knocks, the door will be opened. What father among you, if your son asks for a fish, will give him a snake instead of a fish? Or if he asks for an egg, will give him a scorpion? If you then, although you are evil, know how to give good gifts to your children, how much more will the heavenly Father give the Holy Spirit to those who ask him!"

JESUS AND BEELZEBUL

Now he was casting out a demon that was mute. When the demon had gone out, the man who had been mute began to speak, and the crowds were amazed. But some of them said, "By the power of Beelzebul, the ruler of demons, he casts out demons!" Others, to test him, began asking for a sign from heaven. But Jesus, realizing their thoughts, said to them, "Every kingdom divided against itself is destroyed, and a divided household falls. So if Satan too is divided against himself, how will his kingdom stand? I ask you this because you claim that I cast out demons by Beelzebul. Now if I cast out demons by Beelzebul, by whom do your sons cast them out? Therefore they will be your judges. But if I cast out demons by the finger of God, then the kingdom of God has already overtaken you. When a strong man, fully armed, guards his own palace, his possessions are safe. But when a stronger man attacks and conquers him, he takes away the first man's armor on which the man relied and divides up his plunder. Whoever is not with me is against me, and whoever does not gather with me scatters.

RESPONSE TO JESUS' WORK

"When an unclean spirit goes out of a person, it passes through waterless places looking for rest but not finding any. Then it says, 'I will return to the home I left.' When it returns, it finds the house swept clean and put in order. Then it goes and brings seven other spirits more evil than itself, and they go in and live there, so the last state of that person is worse than the first."

As he said these things, a woman in the crowd spoke out to him, "Blessed is the womb that bore you and the breasts at which you nursed!" But he replied, "Blessed rather are those who hear the word of God and obey it!"

THE SIGN OF JONAH

As the crowds were increasing, Jesus began to say, "This generation is a wicked generation; it looks for a sign, but no sign will be given to it except the sign of Jonah. For just as Jonah became a sign to the people of Nineveh, so the Son of Man will be a sign to this generation. The queen of the South will rise up at the judgment with the people of this generation and condemn them, because she came from the ends of the earth to hear the wisdom of Solomon—and now, something greater than Solomon is here! The people of Nineveh will stand up at the judgment with this generation and condemn it, because they repented when Jonah preached to them—and now, something greater than Jonah is here!

INTERNAL LIGHT

"No one after lighting a lamp puts it in a hidden place or under a basket, but on a lampstand, so that those who come in can see the light. Your eye is the lamp of your body. When your eye is healthy, your whole body is full of light, but when it is diseased, your body is full of darkness. Therefore see to it that the light in you is not darkness. If then your whole body is full of light, with no part in the dark, it will be as full of light as when the light of a lamp shines on you."

REBUKING THE PHARISEES AND EXPERTS IN THE LAW

As he spoke, a Pharisee invited Jesus to have a meal with him, so he went in and took his place at the table. The Pharisee was astonished when he saw that Jesus did not first wash his hands before the meal. But the Lord said to him, "Now you Pharisees clean the outside of the cup and the plate, but inside you are full of greed and wickedness. You fools! Didn't the one who made the outside make the inside as well? But give from your heart to those in need, and then everything will be clean for you.

"But woe to you Pharisees! You give a tenth of your mint, rue, and every herb, yet you neglect justice and love for God! But you should have done these things without neglecting the others. Woe to you Pharisees! You love the best seats in the synagogues and elaborate greetings in the marketplaces! Woe to you! You are like unmarked graves, and people walk over them without realizing it!"

One of the experts in religious law answered him, "Teacher, when you say these things, you insult us too." But Jesus replied, "Woe to you experts in religious law as well! You load people down with burdens difficult to bear, yet you yourselves refuse to touch the burdens with even one of your fingers! Woe to you! You build the tombs of the prophets whom your ancestors killed. So you testify that you approve of the deeds of your ancestors because they killed the prophets and you build their tombs! For this reason also the wisdom of God said, 'I will send them prophets and apostles, some of whom they will kill and persecute,' so that this generation may be held accountable for the blood of all the prophets that has been shed since the beginning of the world, from the blood of Abel to the blood of Zechariah, who was killed between the altar and the sanctuary. Yes, I tell you, it will be charged against this generation. Woe to you experts in religious law! You have taken away the key to knowledge! You did not go in yourselves, and you hindered those who were going in."

When he went out from there, the experts in the law and the Pharisees began to oppose him bitterly and to ask him hostile questions about many things, plotting against him to catch him in something he might say.

CHAPTER 12

FEAR GOD, NOT PEOPLE

Meanwhile, when many thousands of the crowd had gathered so that they were trampling on one another, Jesus began to speak first to his disciples, "Be on your guard against the yeast of the Pharisees, which is hypocrisy. Nothing is hidden that will not be revealed, and nothing is secret that will not be made known. So then whatever you have said in the dark will be heard in the light, and what you have whispered in private rooms will be proclaimed from the housetops.

"I tell you, my friends, do not be afraid of those who kill the body, and after that have nothing more they can do. But I will warn you whom you should fear: Fear the one who, after the killing, has authority to throw you into hell. Yes, I tell you, fear him! Aren't five sparrows sold for two pennies? Yet not one of them is forgotten before God. In fact, even the hairs on your head are all numbered. Do not be afraid; you are more valuable than many sparrows.

"I tell you, whoever acknowledges me before men, the Son of Man will also acknowledge before God's angels. But the one who denies me before men will be denied before God's angels. And everyone who speaks a word against the Son of Man will be forgiven, but the person who blasphemes against the Holy Spirit will not be forgiven. But when they bring you before the synagogues, the rulers, and the authorities, do not worry about how you should make your defense or what you should say, for the Holy Spirit will teach you at that moment what you must say."

THE PARABLE OF THE RICH LANDOWNER

Then someone from the crowd said to him, "Teacher, tell my brother to divide the inheritance with me." But Jesus said to him, "Man, who made me a judge or arbitrator between you two?" Then he said to them, "Watch out and guard yourself from all types of greed because one's life does not consist in the abundance of his possessions." He then told them a parable: "The land of a certain rich man produced an abundant crop, so he thought to himself, 'What should I do, for I have nowhere to store my crops?' Then he said, 'I will do this: I will tear down my barns and build bigger ones, and there I will store all my grain and my goods. And I will say to myself, "You have plenty of goods stored up for many years; relax, eat, drink, celebrate!"' But God said to him, 'You fool! This very night your life will be demanded back from you, but who will get what you have prepared for yourself?' So it is with the one who stores up riches for himself, but is not rich toward God."

EXHORTATION NOT TO WORRY

Then Jesus said to his disciples, "Therefore I tell you, do not worry about your life, what you will eat, or about your body, what you will wear. For there is more to life than food, and more to the body than clothing. Consider the ravens: They do not sow or reap, they have no storeroom or barn, yet God feeds them. How much more valuable are you than the birds! And which of you by worrying can add an hour to his life? So if you cannot do such a very little thing as this, why do you worry about the rest? Consider how the flowers grow; they do not work or spin. Yet I tell you, not even Solomon in all his glory was clothed like one of these! And if this is how God clothes the wild grass, which is here today and tomorrow is tossed into the fire to heat the oven, how much more will he clothe you, you people of little faith! So do not be overly concerned about what you will eat and what you will drink, and do not worry about such things. For all the nations of the world pursue these things, and your Father knows that you need them. Instead, pursue his kingdom, and these things will be given to you as well.

"Do not be afraid, little flock, for your Father is well pleased to give you the kingdom. Sell your possessions and give to the poor. Provide yourselves purses that do not wear out—a treasure in heaven that never decreases, where no thief approaches and no moth destroys. For where your treasure is, there your heart will be also.

CALL TO FAITHFUL STEWARDSHIP

"Get dressed for service and keep your lamps burning; be like people waiting for their master to come back from the wedding celebration, so that when he comes and knocks, they can immediately open the door for him. Blessed are those slaves whom their master finds alert when he returns! I tell you the truth, he will dress himself to serve, have them take their place at the table, and will come and wait on them! Even if he comes in the second or third watch of the night and finds them alert, blessed are those slaves! But understand this: If the owner of the house had known at what hour the thief was coming, he would not have let his house be broken into. You also must be ready because the Son of Man will come at an hour when you do not expect him."

Then Peter said, "Lord, are you telling this parable for us or for everyone?" The Lord replied, "Who then is the faithful and wise manager, whom the master puts in charge of his household servants, to give them their allowance of food at the proper time? Blessed is that slave whom his master finds at work when he returns. I tell you the truth, the master will put him in charge of all his possessions. But if that slave should say to himself, 'My master is delayed in returning,' and he begins to beat the other slaves, both men and women, and to eat, drink, and get drunk, then the master of that slave will come on a day when he does not expect him and at an hour he does not foresee, and will cut him in two, and assign him a place with the unfaithful. That servant who knew his master's will but did not get ready or do what his master asked will receive a severe beating. But the one who did not know his master's will and did things worthy of punishment will receive a light beating. From everyone who has been given much, much will be required, and from the one who has been entrusted with much, even more will be asked.

NOT PEACE, BUT DIVISION

"I have come to bring fire on the earth—and how I wish it were already kindled! I have a baptism to undergo, and how distressed I am until it is finished! Do you think I have come to bring peace on earth? No, I tell you, but rather division! For from now on there will be five in one household divided, three against two and two against three. They will be divided, father against son and son against father, mother against daughter and daughter against mother, mother-in-law against her daughter-in-law and daughter-in-law against mother-in-law."

READING THE SIGNS

Jesus also said to the crowds, "When you see a cloud rising in the west, you say at once, 'A rainstorm is coming,' and it does. And when you see the south wind blowing, you say, 'There will be scorching heat,' and there is. You hypocrites! You know how to interpret the appearance of the earth and the sky, but how can you not know how to interpret the present time?

CLEAR THE DEBTS

"And why don't you judge for yourselves what is right? As you are going with your accuser before the magistrate, make an effort to settle with him on the way, so that he will not drag you before the judge, and the judge hand you over to the officer, and the officer throw you into prison. I tell you, you will never get out of there until you have paid the very last cent!"

CHAPTER 13

A CALL TO REPENT

Now there were some present on that occasion who told him about the Galileans whose blood Pilate had mixed with their sacrifices. He answered them, "Do you think these Galileans were worse sinners than all the other Galileans because they suffered these things? No, I tell you! But unless you repent, you will all perish as well! Or those eighteen who were killed when the tower in Siloam fell on them, do you think they were worse offenders than all the others who live in Jerusalem? No, I tell you! But unless you repent you will all perish as well!"

WARNING TO ISRAEL TO BEAR FRUIT

Then Jesus told this parable: "A man had a fig tree planted in his vineyard, and he came looking for fruit on it and found none. So he said to the worker who tended the vineyard, 'For three years now, I have come looking for fruit on this fig tree, and each time I inspect it I find none. Cut it down! Why should it continue to deplete the soil?' But the worker answered him, 'Sir, leave it alone this year too, until I dig around it and put fertilizer on it. Then if it bears fruit next year, very well, but if not, you can cut it down.' "

HEALING ON THE SABBATH

Now he was teaching in one of the synagogues on the Sabbath, and a woman was there who had been disabled by a spirit for eighteen years. She was bent over and could not straighten herself up completely. When Jesus saw her, he called her to him and said, "Woman, you are freed from your infirmity." Then he placed his hands on her, and immediately she straightened up and praised God. But the president of the synagogue, indignant because Jesus had healed on the Sabbath, said to the crowd, "There are six days on which work should be done! So come and be healed on those days, and not on the Sabbath day." Then the Lord answered him, "You hypocrites! Does not each of you on the Sabbath untie his ox or his donkey from its stall and lead it to water? Then shouldn't this woman, a daughter of Abraham whom Satan bound for eighteen long years, be released from this imprisonment on the Sabbath day?" When he said this, all his adversaries were humiliated, but the entire crowd was rejoicing at all the wonderful things he was doing.

ON THE KINGDOM OF GOD

Thus Jesus asked, "What is the kingdom of God like? To what should I compare it? It is like a mustard seed that a man took and sowed in his garden. It grew and became a tree, and the wild birds nested in its branches."

Again he said, "To what should I compare the kingdom of God? It is like yeast that a woman took and mixed with three measures of flour until all the dough had risen."

THE NARROW DOOR

Then Jesus traveled throughout towns and villages, teaching and making his way toward Jerusalem. Someone asked him, "Lord, will only a few be saved?" So he said to them, "Exert every effort to enter through the narrow door because many, I tell you, will try to enter and will not be able to. Once the head of the house gets up and shuts the door, then you will stand outside and start to knock on the door and beg him, 'Lord, let us in!' But he will answer you, 'I don't know where you come from.' Then you will begin to say, 'We ate and drank in your presence, and you taught in our streets.' But he will reply, 'I don't know where you come from! Go away from me, all you evildoers!' There will be weeping and gnashing of teeth when you see Abraham, Isaac, Jacob, and all the prophets in the kingdom of God but you yourselves thrown out. Then people will come from east and west, and from north and south, and take their places at the banquet table in the kingdom of God. But indeed, some are last who will be first, and some are first who will be last."

GOING TO JERUSALEM

At that time, some Pharisees came up and said to Jesus, "Get away from here because Herod wants to kill you." But he said to them, "Go and tell that fox, 'Look, I am casting out demons and performing healings today and tomorrow, and on the third day I will complete my work. Nevertheless I must go on my way today and tomorrow and the next day, because it is impossible that a prophet should be killed outside Jerusalem.' O Jerusalem, Jerusalem, you who kill the prophets and stone those who are sent to you! How often I have longed to gather your children together as a hen gathers her chicks under her wings, but you would have none of it! Look, your house is forsaken! And I tell you, you will not see me until you say, *'Blessed is the one who comes in the name of the Lord!'* "

CHAPTER 14

HEALING AGAIN ON THE SABBATH

Now one Sabbath when Jesus went to dine at the house of a leader of the Pharisees, they were watching him closely. There right in front of him was a man whose body was swollen with fluid. So Jesus asked the experts in religious law and the Pharisees, "Is it lawful to heal on the Sabbath or not?" But they remained silent. So Jesus took hold of the man, healed him, and sent him away. Then he said to them, "Which of you, if you have a son or an ox that has fallen into a well on a Sabbath day, will not immediately pull him out?" But they could not reply to this.

ON SEEKING SEATS OF HONOR

Then when Jesus noticed how the guests chose the places of honor, he told them a parable. He said to them, "When you are invited by someone to a wedding feast, do not take the place of honor because a person more distinguished than you may have been invited by your host. So the host who invited both of you will come and say to you, 'Give this man your place.' Then, ashamed, you will begin to move to the least important place. But when you are invited, go and take the least important place, so that when your host approaches he will say to you, 'Friend, move up here to a better place.' Then you will be honored in the presence of all who share the meal with you. For everyone who exalts himself will be humbled, but the one who humbles himself will be exalted."

He said also to the man who had invited him, "When you host a dinner or a banquet, don't invite your friends or your brothers or your relatives or rich neighbors so you can be invited by them in return and get repaid. But when you host an elaborate meal, invite the poor, the crippled, the lame, and the blind. Then you will be blessed because they cannot repay you, for you will be repaid at the resurrection of the righteous."

THE PARABLE OF THE GREAT BANQUET

When one of those at the meal with Jesus heard this, he said to him, "Blessed is everyone who will feast in the kingdom of God!" But Jesus said to him, "A man once gave a great banquet and invited many guests. At the time for the banquet he sent his slave to tell those who had been invited, 'Come, because everything is now ready.' But one after another they all began to make excuses. The first said to him, 'I have bought a field, and I must go out and see it. Please excuse me.' Another said, 'I have bought five yoke of oxen, and I am going out to examine them. Please excuse me.' Another said, 'I just got married, and I cannot come.' So the slave came back and reported this to his master. Then the master of the household was furious and said to his slave, 'Go out quickly to the streets and alleys of the city, and bring in the poor, the crippled, the blind, and the lame.' Then the slave said, 'Sir, what you instructed has been done, and there is still room.' So the master said to his slave, 'Go out to the highways and country roads and urge people to come in, so that my house will be filled. For I tell you, not one of those individuals who were invited will taste my banquet!' "

COUNTING THE COST

Now large crowds were accompanying Jesus, and turning to them he said, "If anyone comes to me and does not hate his own father and mother, and wife and children, and brothers and sisters, and even his own life, he cannot be my disciple. Whoever does not carry his own cross and follow me cannot be my disciple. For which of you, wanting to build a tower, doesn't sit down first and compute the cost to see if he has enough money to complete it? Otherwise, when he has laid a foundation and is not able to finish the tower, all who see it will begin to make fun of him. They will say, 'This man began to build and was not able to finish!' Or what king, going out to confront another king in battle, will not sit down first and determine whether he is able with 10,000 to oppose the one coming against him with 20,000? If he cannot succeed, he will send a representative while the other is still a long way off and ask for terms of peace. In the same way therefore not one of you can be my disciple if he does not renounce all his own possessions.

"Salt is good, but if salt loses its flavor, how can its flavor be restored? It is of no value for the soil or for the manure pile; it is to be thrown out. The one who has ears to hear had better listen!"

CHAPTER 15

THE PARABLE OF THE LOST SHEEP AND COIN

Now all the tax collectors and sinners were coming to hear him. But the Pharisees and the experts in the law were complaining, "This man welcomes sinners and eats with them."

So Jesus told them this parable: "Which one of you, if he has a hundred sheep and loses one of them, would not leave the ninety-nine in the open pasture and go look for the one that is lost until he finds it? Then when he has found it, he places it on his shoulders, rejoicing. Returning home, he calls together his friends and neighbors, telling them, 'Rejoice with me because I have found my sheep that was lost.' I tell you, in the same way there will be more joy in heaven over one sinner who repents than over ninety-nine righteous people who have no need to repent.

"Or what woman, if she has ten silver coins and loses one of them, does not light a lamp, sweep the house, and search thoroughly until she finds it? Then when she has found it, she calls together her friends and neighbors, saying, 'Rejoice with me, for I have found the coin that I had lost.' In the same way, I tell you, there is joy in the presence of God's angels over one sinner who repents."

THE PARABLE OF THE COMPASSIONATE FATHER
Then Jesus said, "A man had two sons. The younger of them said to his father, 'Father, give me the share of the estate that will belong to me.' So he divided his assets between them. After a few days, the younger son gathered together all he had and left on a journey to a distant country, and there he squandered his wealth with a wild lifestyle. Then after he had spent everything, a severe famine took place in that country, and he began to be in need. So he went and worked for one of the citizens

of that country, who sent him to his fields to feed pigs. He was longing to eat the carob pods the pigs were eating, but no one gave him anything. But when he came to his senses, he said, 'How many of my father's hired workers have food enough to spare, but here I am dying from hunger! I will get up and go to my father and say to him, "Father, I have sinned against heaven and against you. I am no longer worthy to be called your son; treat me like one of your hired workers." ' So he got up and went to his father. But while he was still a long way from home his father saw him, and his heart went out to him; he ran and hugged his son and kissed him. Then his son said to him, 'Father, I have sinned against heaven and against you; I am no longer worthy to be called your son.' But the father said to his slaves, 'Hurry! Bring the best robe, and put it on him! Put a ring on his finger and sandals on his feet! Bring the fattened calf and kill it! Let us eat and celebrate, because this son of mine was dead, and is alive again—he was lost and is found!' So they began to celebrate.

"Now his older son was in the field. As he came and approached the house, he heard music and dancing. So he called one of the slaves and asked what was happening. The slave replied, 'Your brother has returned, and your father has killed the fattened calf because he got his son back safe and sound.' But the older son became angry and refused to go in. His father came out and appealed to him, but he answered his father, 'Look! These many years I have worked like a slave for you, and I never disobeyed your commands. Yet you never gave me even a goat so that I could celebrate with my friends! But when this son of yours came back, who has devoured your assets with prostitutes, you killed the fattened calf for him!' Then the father said to him, 'Son, you are always with me, and everything that belongs to me is yours. It was appropriate to celebrate and be glad, for your brother was dead, and is alive; he was lost and is found.'"

CHAPTER 16

THE PARABLE OF THE CLEVER STEWARD

Jesus also said to the disciples, "There was a rich man who was informed of accusations that his manager was wasting his assets. So he called the manager in and said to him, 'What is this I hear about you? Turn in the account of your administration, because you can no longer be my manager.' Then the manager said to himself, 'What should I do, since my master is taking my position away from me? I'm not strong enough to dig, and I'm too ashamed to beg. I know what to do so that when I am put out of management, people will welcome me into their homes.' So he contacted his master's debtors one by one. He asked the first, 'How much do you owe my master?' The man replied, '100 measures of olive oil.' The manager said to him, 'Take your bill, sit down quickly, and write 50.' Then he said to another, 'And how much do you owe?' The second man replied, '100 measures of wheat.' The manager said to him, 'Take your bill, and write 80.' The master commended the dishonest manager because he acted shrewdly. For the people of this world are more shrewd in dealing with their contemporaries than the people of light. And I tell you, make friends for yourselves by how you use worldly wealth, so that when it runs out, you will be welcomed into the eternal homes.

"The one who is faithful in a very little is also faithful in much, and the one who is dishonest in a very little is also dishonest in much. If then you haven't been trustworthy in handling worldly wealth, who will entrust you with the true riches? And if you haven't been trustworthy with someone else's property, who will give you your own? No servant can serve two masters, for either he will hate the one and love the other, or he will be devoted to the one and despise the other. You cannot serve God and money."

MORE WARNINGS ABOUT THE PHARISEES

The Pharisees (who loved money) heard all this and ridiculed him. But Jesus said to them, "You are the ones who justify yourselves in men's eyes, but God knows your hearts. For what is highly prized among men is utterly detestable in God's sight.

"The law and the prophets were in force until John; since then, the good news of the kingdom of God has been proclaimed, and everyone is urged to enter it. But it is easier for heaven and earth to pass away than for one tiny stroke of a letter in the law to become void.

"Everyone who divorces his wife and marries someone else commits adultery, and the one who marries a woman divorced from her husband commits adultery.

THE RICH MAN AND LAZARUS

"There was a rich man who dressed in purple and fine linen and who feasted sumptuously every day. But at his gate lay a poor man named Lazarus whose body was covered with sores, who longed to eat what fell from the rich man's table. In addition, the dogs came and licked his sores.

"Now the poor man died and was carried by the angels to Abraham's side. The rich man also died and was buried. And in Hades, as he was in torment, he looked up and saw Abraham far off with Lazarus at his side. So he called out, 'Father Abraham, have mercy on me, and send Lazarus to dip the tip of his finger in water and cool my tongue because I am in anguish in this fire.' But Abraham said, 'Child, remember that in your lifetime you received your good things and Lazarus likewise bad things, but now he is comforted here and you are in anguish. Besides all this, a great chasm has been fixed between us, so that those who want to cross over from here to you cannot do so, and no one can cross from there to us.' So the rich man said, 'Then I beg you, father—send Lazarus to my father's house (for I have five brothers) to warn them so that they don't come into this place of torment.' But Abraham said, 'They have Moses and the prophets; they must respond to them.' Then the rich man said, 'No, father Abraham, but if someone from the dead goes to them, they will repent.' He replied to him, 'If they do not respond to Moses and the prophets, they will not be convinced even if someone rises from the dead.'"

CHAPTER 17

SIN, FORGIVENESS, FAITH, AND SERVICE

Jesus said to his disciples, "Stumbling blocks are sure to come, but woe to the one through whom they come! It would be better for him to have a millstone tied around his neck and be thrown into the sea than for him to cause one of these little ones to sin. Watch yourselves! If your brother sins, rebuke him. If he repents, forgive him. Even if he sins against you seven times in a day, and seven times returns to you saying, 'I repent,' you must forgive him."

The apostles said to the Lord, "Increase our faith!" So the Lord replied, "If you had faith the size of a mustard seed, you could say to this black mulberry tree, 'Be pulled out by the roots and planted in the sea,' and it would obey you.

"Would any one of you say to your slave who comes in from the field after plowing or shepherding sheep, 'Come at once and sit down for a meal'? Won't the master instead say to him, 'Get my dinner ready, and make yourself ready to serve me while I eat and drink. Then you may eat and drink'? He won't thank the slave because he did what he was told, will he? So you too, when you have done everything you were commanded to do, should say, 'We are slaves undeserving of special praise; we have only done what was our duty.'"

THE GRATEFUL LEPER

Now on the way to Jerusalem, Jesus was passing along between Samaria and Galilee. As he was entering a village, ten men with leprosy met him. They stood at a distance, raised their voices and said, "Jesus, Master, have mercy on us." When he saw them he said, "Go and show yourselves to the priests." And as they went along, they were cleansed. Then one of them, when he saw he was healed, turned back, praising God with a loud voice. He fell with his face to the ground at Jesus' feet and thanked him. (Now he was a Samaritan.) Then Jesus said, "Were not ten cleansed? Where are the other nine? Was no one found to turn back and give praise to God except this foreigner?" Then he said to the man, "Get up and go your way. Your faith has made you well."

THE COMING OF THE KINGDOM

Now at one point the Pharisees asked Jesus when the kingdom of God was coming, so he answered, "The kingdom of God is not coming with signs to be observed, nor will they say, 'Look, here it is!' or 'There!' For indeed, the kingdom of God is in your midst."

THE COMING OF THE SON OF MAN

Then he said to the disciples, "The days are coming when you will desire to see one of the days of the Son of Man, and you will not see it. Then people will say to you, 'Look, there he is!' or 'Look, here he is!' Do not go out or chase after them. For just like the lightning flashes and lights up the sky from one side to the other, so will the Son of Man be in his day. But first he must suffer many things and be rejected by this generation. Just as it was in the days of Noah, so too it will be in the days of the Son of Man. People were eating, they were drinking, they were marrying, they were being given in marriage—right up to the day Noah entered the ark. Then the flood came and destroyed them all. Likewise, just as it was in the days of Lot, people were eating, drinking, buying, selling, planting, building; but on the day Lot went out from Sodom, fire and sulfur rained down from heaven and destroyed them all. It will be the same on the day the Son of Man is revealed. On that day, anyone who is on the roof, with his goods in the house, must not come down to take them away, and likewise the person in the field must not turn back. Remember Lot's wife! Whoever tries to keep his life will lose it, but whoever loses his life will preserve it. I tell you, in that night there will be two people in one bed; one will be taken and the other left. There will be two women grinding grain together; one will be taken and the other left."

Then the disciples said to him, "Where, Lord?" He replied to them, "Where the dead body is, there the vultures will gather."

CHAPTER 18

PRAYER AND THE PARABLE
OF THE PERSISTENT WIDOW

Then Jesus told them a parable to show them they should always pray and not lose heart. He said, "In a certain city there was a judge who neither feared God nor respected people. There was also a widow in that city who kept coming to him and saying, 'Give me justice against my adversary.' For a while he refused, but later on he said to himself, 'Though I neither fear God nor have regard for people, yet because this widow keeps on bothering me, I will give her justice, or in the end she will wear me out by her unending pleas.'" And the Lord said, "Listen to what the unrighteous judge says! Won't God give justice to his chosen ones, who cry out to him day and night? Will he delay long to help them? I tell you, he will give them justice speedily. Nevertheless, when the Son of Man comes, will he find faith on earth?"

THE PARABLE OF THE PHARISEE AND TAX COLLECTOR

Jesus also told this parable to some who were confident that they were righteous and looked down on everyone else. "Two men went up to the temple to pray, one a Pharisee and the other a tax collector. The Pharisee stood and prayed about himself like this: 'God, I thank you that I am not like other people: extortionists, unrighteous people, adulterers—or even like this tax collector. I fast twice a week; I give a tenth of everything I get.' The tax collector, however, stood far off and would not even look up to heaven, but beat his breast and said, 'God, be merciful to me, sinner that I am!' I tell you that this man went down to his home justified rather than the Pharisee. For everyone who exalts himself will be humbled, but he who humbles himself will be exalted."

JESUS AND LITTLE CHILDREN

Now people were even bringing their babies to him for him to touch. But when the disciples saw it, they began to scold those who brought them. But Jesus called for the children, saying, "Let the little children come to me and do not try to stop them, for the kingdom of God belongs to such as these. I tell you the truth, whoever does not receive the kingdom of God like a child will never enter it."

THE WEALTHY RULER

Now a certain leader asked him, "Good teacher, what must I do to inherit eternal life?" Jesus said to him, "Why do you call me good? No one is good except God alone. You know the commandments: *'Do not commit adultery, do not murder, do not steal, do not give false testimony, honor your father and mother.'* " The man replied, "I have wholeheartedly obeyed all these laws since my youth." When Jesus heard this, he said to him, "One thing you still lack. Sell all that you have and give the money to the poor, and you will have treasure in heaven. Then come, follow me." But when the man heard this, he became very sad, for he was extremely wealthy. When Jesus noticed this, he said, "How hard it is for the rich to enter the kingdom of God! In fact, it is easier for a camel to go through the eye of a needle than for a rich person to enter the kingdom of God." Those who heard this said, "Then who can be saved?" He replied, "What is impossible for mere humans is possible for God." And Peter said, "Look, we have left everything we own to follow you!" Then Jesus said to them, "I tell you the truth, there is no one who has left home or wife or brothers or parents or children for the sake of God's kingdom who will not receive many times more in this age—and in the age to come, eternal life."

ANOTHER PREDICTION OF JESUS' PASSION

Then Jesus took the twelve aside and said to them, "Look, we are going up to Jerusalem, and everything that is written about the Son of Man by the prophets will be accomplished. For he will be handed over to the Gentiles; he will be mocked, mistreated, and spat on. They will flog him severely and kill him. Yet on the third day he will rise again." But the twelve understood none of these things. This saying was hidden from them, and they did not grasp what Jesus meant.

HEALING A BLIND MAN

As Jesus approached Jericho, a blind man was sitting by the road begging. When he heard a crowd going by, he asked what was going on. They told him, "Jesus the Nazarene is passing by." So he called out, "Jesus, Son of David, have mercy on me!" And those who were in front scolded him to get him to be quiet, but he shouted even more, "Son of David, have mercy on me!" So Jesus stopped and ordered the beggar to be brought to him. When the man came near, Jesus asked him, "What do you want me to do for you?" He replied, "Lord, let me see again." Jesus said to him, "Receive your sight; your faith has healed you." And immediately he regained his sight and followed Jesus, praising God. When all the people saw it, they too gave praise to God.

CHAPTER 19

JESUS AND ZACCHAEUS

Jesus entered Jericho and was passing through it. Now a man named Zacchaeus was there; he was a chief tax collector and was rich. He was trying to get a look at Jesus, but being a short man he could not see over the crowd. So he ran on ahead and climbed up into a sycamore tree to see him because Jesus was going to pass that way. And when Jesus came to that place, he looked up and said to him, "Zacchaeus, come down quickly because I must stay at your house today." So he came down quickly and welcomed Jesus joyfully. And when the people saw it, they all complained, "He has gone in to be the guest of a man who is a sinner." But Zacchaeus stopped and said to the Lord, "Look, Lord, half of my possessions I now give to the poor, and if I have cheated anyone of anything, I am paying back four times as much!" Then Jesus said to him, "Today salvation has come to this household because he too is a son of Abraham! For the Son of Man came to seek and to save the lost."

THE PARABLE OF THE TEN MINAS

While the people were listening to these things, Jesus proceeded to tell a parable because he was near to Jerusalem, and because they thought that the kingdom of God was going to appear immediately. Therefore he said, "A nobleman went to a distant country to receive for himself a kingdom and then return. And he summoned ten of his slaves, gave them ten minas, and said to them, 'Do business with these until I come back.' But his citizens hated him and sent a delegation after him, saying, 'We do not want this man to be king over us!' When he returned after receiving the kingdom, he summoned these slaves to whom he had given the money. He wanted to know how much they had earned by trading. So the first one came before him and said, 'Sir, your mina has made ten minas more.' And the king said to him, 'Well done, good slave! Because you have been faithful in a very small matter, you will have authority over ten cities.' Then the second one came and said, 'Sir, your mina has made five minas.' So the king said to him, 'And you are to be over five cities.' Then another slave came and said, 'Sir, here is your mina that I put away for safekeeping in a piece of cloth. For I was afraid of you because you are a severe man. You withdraw what you did not deposit and reap what you did not sow.' The king said to him, 'I will judge you by your own words, you wicked slave! So you knew, did you, that I was a severe man, withdrawing what I didn't deposit and reaping what I didn't sow? Why then didn't you put my money in the bank, so that when I returned I could have collected it with interest?' And he said to his attendants, 'Take the mina from him, and give it to the one who has ten.' But they said to him, 'Sir, he has ten minas already!' 'I tell you that everyone who has will be given more, but from the one who does not have, even what he has will be taken away. But as for these enemies of mine who did not want me to be their king, bring them here and slaughter them in front of me!' "

THE TRIUMPHAL ENTRY

After Jesus had said this, he continued on ahead, going up to Jerusalem. Now when he approached Bethphage and Bethany, at the place called the Mount of Olives, he sent two of the disciples, telling them, "Go to the village ahead of you. When you enter it, you will find a colt tied there that has never been ridden. Untie it and bring it here. If anyone asks you, 'Why are you untying it?' just say, 'The Lord needs it.' " So those who were sent ahead found it exactly as he had told them. As they were untying the colt, its owners asked them, "Why are you untying that colt?" They replied, "The Lord needs it." Then they brought it to Jesus, threw their cloaks on the colt, and had Jesus get on it. As he rode along, they spread their cloaks on the road. As he approached the road leading down from the Mount of Olives, the whole crowd of his disciples began to rejoice and praise God with a loud voice for all the mighty works they had seen: *"Blessed is the king who comes in the name of the Lord!* Peace in heaven and glory in the highest!" But some of the Pharisees in the crowd said to him, "Teacher, rebuke your disciples." He answered, "I tell you, if they keep silent, the very stones will cry out!"

JESUS WEEPS FOR JERUSALEM UNDER JUDGMENT

Now when Jesus approached and saw the city, he wept over it, saying, "If you had only known on this day, even you, the things that make for peace! But now they are hidden from your eyes. For the days will come upon you when your enemies will build an embankment against you and surround you and close in on you from every side. They will demolish you—you and your children within your walls—and they will not leave within you one stone on top of another because you did not recognize the time of your visitation from God."

CLEANSING THE TEMPLE

Then Jesus entered the temple courts and began to drive out those who were selling things there, saying to them, "It is written, *'My house will be a house of prayer,'* but you have turned it into *a den of robbers*!"

Jesus was teaching daily in the temple courts. The chief priests and the experts in the law and the prominent leaders among the people were seeking to assassinate him, but they could not find a way to do it, for all the people hung on his words.

CHAPTER 20

THE AUTHORITY OF JESUS

Now one day, as Jesus was teaching the people in the temple courts and proclaiming the gospel, the chief priests and the experts in the law with the elders came up and said to him, "Tell us: By what authority are you doing these things? Or who is it who gave you this authority?" He answered them, "I will also ask you a question, and you tell me: John's baptism—was it from heaven or from people?" So they discussed it with one another, saying, "If we say, 'From heaven,' he will say, 'Why did you not believe him?' But if we say, 'From people,' all the people will stone us because they are convinced that John was a prophet." So they replied that they did not know where it came from. Then Jesus said to them, "Neither will I tell you by whose authority I do these things."

THE PARABLE OF THE TENANTS

Then he began to tell the people this parable: "A man planted a vineyard, leased it to tenant farmers, and went on a journey for a long time. When harvest time came, he sent a slave to the tenants so that they would give him his portion of the crop. However, the tenants beat his slave and sent him away empty-handed. So he sent another slave. They beat this one too, treated him outrageously, and sent him away empty-handed. So he sent still a third. They even wounded this one and threw him out. Then the owner of the vineyard said, 'What should I do? I will send my one dear son; perhaps they will respect him.' But when the tenants saw him, they said to one another, 'This is the heir; let's kill him so the inheritance will be ours!' So they threw him out of the vineyard and killed him. What then will the owner of the vineyard do to them? He will come and destroy those tenants and give the vineyard to others." When the people heard this, they said, "May this never happen!" But Jesus looked straight at them and said, "Then what is the meaning of that which is written: *'The stone the builders rejected has become the cornerstone'*? Everyone who falls on this stone will be broken to pieces, and the one on whom it falls will be crushed." Then the experts in the law and the chief priests wanted to arrest him that very hour because they realized he had told this parable against them. But they were afraid of the people.

PAYING TAXES TO CAESAR

Then they watched him carefully and sent spies who pretended to be sincere. They wanted to take advantage of what he might say so that they could deliver him up to the authority and jurisdiction of the governor. Thus they asked him, "Teacher, we know that you speak and teach correctly, and show no partiality, but teach the way of God in accordance with the truth. Is it right for us to pay the tribute tax to Caesar or not?" But Jesus perceived their deceit and said to them, "Show me a denarius. Whose image and inscription are on it?" They said, "Caesar's." So he said to them, "Then give to Caesar the things that are Caesar's, and to God the things that are God's." Thus they were unable in the presence of the people to trap him with his own words. And stunned by his answer, they fell silent.

MARRIAGE AND THE RESURRECTION

Now some Sadducees (who contend that there is no resurrection) came to him. They asked him, "Teacher, Moses wrote for us that *if a man's brother dies leaving* a wife but *no children, that man must marry the widow and father children for his brother.* Now there were seven brothers. The first one married a woman and died without children. The second and then the third married her, and in this same way all seven died, leaving no children. Finally the woman died too. In the resurrection, therefore, whose wife will the woman be? For all seven had married her."

So Jesus said to them, "The people of this age marry and are given in marriage. But those who are regarded as worthy to share in that age and in the resurrection from the dead neither marry nor are given in marriage. In fact, they can no longer die because they are equal to angels and are sons of God, since they are sons of the resurrection. But even Moses revealed that the dead are raised in the passage about the bush, where he calls the Lord *the God of Abraham and the God of Isaac and the God of Jacob.* Now he is not God of the dead, but of the living, for all live before him." Then some of the experts in the law answered, "Teacher, you have spoken well!" For they did not dare any longer to ask him anything.

THE MESSIAH: DAVID'S SON AND LORD

But he said to them, "How is it that they say that the Christ is David's son? For David himself says in the book of Psalms,

'The Lord said to my lord,
"Sit at my right hand,
until I make your enemies a footstool for
your feet."'

If David then calls him 'Lord,' how can he be his son?"

JESUS WARNS THE DISCIPLES
AGAINST PRIDE

As all the people were listening, Jesus said to his disciples, "Beware of the experts in the law. They like walking around in long robes, and they love elaborate greetings in the marketplaces and the best seats in the synagogues and the places of honor at banquets. They devour widows' property, and as a show make long prayers. They will receive a more severe punishment."

CHAPTER 21

THE WIDOW'S OFFERING

Jesus looked up and saw the rich putting their gifts into the offering box. He also saw a poor widow put in two small copper coins. He said, "I tell you the truth, this poor widow has put in more than all of them. For they all offered their gifts out of their wealth. But she, out of her poverty, put in everything she had to live on."

THE SIGNS OF THE END OF THE AGE

Now while some were speaking about the temple, how it was adorned with beautiful stones and offerings, Jesus said, "As for these things that you are gazing at, the days will come when not one stone will be left on another. All will be torn down!" So they asked him, "Teacher, when will these things happen? And what will be the sign that these things are about to take place?" He said, "Watch out that you are not misled. For many will come in my name, saying, 'I am he,' and, 'The time is near.' Do not follow them! And when you hear of wars and rebellions, do not be afraid. For these things must happen first, but the end will not come at once."

PERSECUTION OF DISCIPLES

Then he said to them, "Nation will rise up in arms against nation, and kingdom against kingdom. There will be great earthquakes, and famines and plagues in various places, and there will be terrifying sights and great signs from heaven. But before all this, they will seize you and persecute you, handing you over to the synagogues and prisons. You will be brought before kings and governors because of my name. This will be a time for you to serve as witnesses. Therefore be resolved not to rehearse ahead of time how to make your defense. For I will give you the words along with the wisdom that none of your adversaries will be able to withstand or contradict. You will be betrayed even by parents, brothers, relatives, and friends, and they will have some of you put to death. You will be hated by everyone because of my name. Yet not a hair of your head will perish. By your endurance you will gain your lives.

THE DESOLATION OF JERUSALEM

"But when you see Jerusalem surrounded by armies, then know that its desolation has come near. Then those who are in Judea must flee to the mountains. Those who are inside the city must depart. Those who are out in the country must not enter it, because these are days of vengeance, to fulfill all that is written. Woe to those who are pregnant and to those who are nursing their babies in those days! For there will be great distress on the earth and wrath against this people. They will fall by the edge of the sword and be led away as captives among all nations. Jerusalem will be trampled down by the Gentiles until the times of the Gentiles are fulfilled.

THE ARRIVAL OF THE SON OF MAN

"And there will be signs in the sun and moon and stars, and on the earth nations will be in distress, anxious over the roaring of the sea and the surging waves. People will be fainting from fear and from the expectation of what is coming on the world, for *the powers of the heavens will be shaken*. Then they will see *the Son of Man arriving in a cloud* with power and great glory. But when these things begin to happen, stand up and raise your heads because your redemption is drawing near."

THE PARABLE OF THE FIG TREE

Then he told them a parable: "Look at the fig tree and all the other trees. When they sprout leaves, you see for yourselves and know that summer is now near. So also you, when you see these things happening, know that the kingdom of God is near. I tell you the truth, this generation will not pass away until all these things take place. Heaven and earth will pass away, but my words will never pass away.

BE READY!

"But be on your guard so that your hearts are not weighed down with dissipation and drunkenness and the worries of this life, and that day close down upon you suddenly like a trap. For it will overtake all who live on the face of the whole earth. But stay alert at all times, praying that you may have strength to escape all these things that must happen, and to stand before the Son of Man."

So every day Jesus was teaching in the temple courts, but at night he went and stayed on the Mount of Olives. And all the people came to him early in the morning to listen to him in the temple courts.

CHAPTER 22

JUDAS' DECISION TO BETRAY JESUS

Now the Feast of Unleavened Bread, which is called the Passover, was approaching. The chief priests and the experts in the law were trying to find some way to execute Jesus, for they were afraid of the people.

Then Satan entered Judas, the one called Iscariot, who was one of the twelve. He went away and discussed with the chief priests and officers of the temple guard how he might betray Jesus, handing him over to them. They were delighted and arranged to give him money. So Judas agreed and began looking for an opportunity to betray Jesus when no crowd was present.

THE PASSOVER

Then the day for the feast of Unleavened Bread came, on which the Passover lamb had to be sacrificed. Jesus sent Peter and John, saying, "Go and prepare the Passover for us to eat." They said to him, "Where do you want us to prepare it?" He said to them, "Listen, when you have entered the city, a man carrying a jar of water will meet you. Follow him into the house that he enters, and tell the owner of the house, 'The Teacher says to you, "Where is the guest room where I may eat the Passover with my disciples?" ' Then he will show you a large furnished room upstairs. Make preparations there." So they went and found things just as he had told them, and they prepared the Passover.

THE LORD'S SUPPER

Now when the hour came, Jesus took his place at the table and the apostles joined him. And he said to them, "I have earnestly desired to eat this Passover with you before I suffer. For I tell you, I will not eat it again until it is fulfilled in the kingdom of God." Then he took a cup, and after giving thanks he said, "Take this and divide it among yourselves. For I tell you that from now on I will not drink of the fruit of the vine until the kingdom of God comes." Then he took bread, and after giving thanks he broke it and gave it to them, saying, "This is my body which is given for you. Do this in remembrance of me." And in the same way he took the cup after they had eaten, saying, "This cup that is poured out for you is the new covenant in my blood.

A FINAL DISCOURSE

"But look, the hand of the one who betrays me is with me on the table. For the Son of Man is to go just as it has been determined, but woe to that man by whom he is betrayed!" So they began to question one another as to which of them it could possibly be who would do this.

A dispute also started among them over which of them was to be regarded as the greatest. So Jesus said to them, "The kings of the Gentiles lord it over them, and those in authority over them are called 'benefactors.' Not so with you; instead the one who is greatest among you must become like the youngest, and the leader like the one who serves. For who is greater, the one who is seated at the table, or the one who serves? Is it not the one who is seated at the table? But I am among you as one who serves.

"You are the ones who have remained with me in my trials. Thus I grant to you a kingdom, just as my Father granted to me, that you may eat and drink at my table in my kingdom, and you will sit on thrones judging the 12 tribes of Israel.

"Simon, Simon, pay attention! Satan has demanded to have you all, to sift you like wheat, but I have prayed for you, Simon, that your faith may not fail. When you have turned back, strengthen your brothers." But Peter said to him, "Lord, I am ready to go with you both to prison and to death!" Jesus replied, "I tell you, Peter, the rooster will not crow today until you have denied three times that you know me."

Then Jesus said to them, "When I sent you out with no money bag, or traveler's bag, or sandals, you didn't lack anything, did you?" They replied, "Nothing." He said to them, "But now, the one who has a money bag must take it, and likewise a traveler's bag too. And the one who has no sword must sell his cloak and buy one. For I tell you that this scripture must be fulfilled in me, '*And he was counted with the transgressors.*' For what is written about me is being fulfilled." So they said, "Look, Lord, here are two swords." Then he told them, "It is enough."

ON THE MOUNT OF OLIVES

Then Jesus went out and made his way, as he customarily did, to the Mount of Olives, and the disciples followed him. When he came to the place, he said to them, "Pray that you will not fall into temptation." He went away from them about a stone's throw, knelt down, and prayed, "Father, if you are willing, take this cup away from me. Yet not my will but yours be done." [Then an angel from heaven appeared to him and strengthened him. And in his anguish he prayed more earnestly, and his sweat was like drops of blood falling to the ground.] When he got up from prayer, he came to the disciples and found them sleeping, exhausted from grief. So he said to them, "Why are you sleeping? Get up and pray that you will not fall into temptation!"

BETRAYAL AND ARREST

While he was still speaking, suddenly a crowd appeared, and the man named Judas, one of the twelve, was leading them. He walked up to Jesus to kiss him. But Jesus said to him, "Judas, would you betray the Son of Man with a kiss?" When those who were around him saw what was about to happen, they said, "Lord, should we use our swords?" Then one of them struck the high priest's slave, cutting off his right ear. But Jesus said, "Enough of this!" And he touched the man's ear and healed him. Then Jesus said to the chief priests, the officers of the temple guard, and the elders who had come out to get him, "Have you come out with swords and clubs like you would against an outlaw? Day after day when I was with you in the temple courts, you did not arrest me. But this is your hour, and that of the power of darkness!"

JESUS' CONDEMNATION
AND PETER'S DENIALS

Then they arrested Jesus, led him away, and brought him into the high priest's house. But Peter was following at a distance. When they had made a fire in the middle of the courtyard and sat down together, Peter sat down among them. Then a slave girl, seeing him as he sat in the firelight, stared at him and said, "This man was with him too!" But Peter denied it: "Woman, I don't know him!" Then a little later someone else saw him and said, "You are one of them too." But Peter said, "Man, I am not!" And after about an hour still another insisted, "Certainly this man was with him because he too is a Galilean." But Peter said, "Man, I don't know what you're talking about!" At that moment, while he was still speaking, a rooster crowed. Then the Lord turned and looked straight at Peter, and Peter remembered the word of the Lord, how he had said to him, "Before a rooster crows today, you will deny me three times." And he went outside and wept bitterly.

Now the men who were holding Jesus under guard began to mock him and beat him. They blindfolded him and asked him repeatedly, "Prophesy! Who hit you?" They also said many other things against him, reviling him.

When day came, the council of the elders of the people gathered together, both the chief priests and the experts in the law. Then they led Jesus away to their council and said, "If you are the Christ, tell us." But he said to them, "If I tell you, you will not believe, and if I ask you, you will not answer. But from now on *the Son of Man will be seated at the right hand* of the power of God." So they all said, "Are you the Son of God, then?" He answered them, "You say that I am." Then they said, "Why do we need further testimony? We have heard it ourselves from his own lips!"

CHAPTER 23

JESUS BROUGHT BEFORE PILATE

Then the whole group of them rose up and brought Jesus before Pilate. They began to accuse him, saying, "We found this man subverting our nation, forbidding us to pay the tribute tax to Caesar and claiming that he himself is Christ, a king." So Pilate asked Jesus, "Are you the king of the Jews?" He replied, "You say so." Then Pilate said to the chief priests and the crowds, "I find no basis for an accusation against this man." But they persisted in saying, "He incites the people by teaching throughout all Judea. It started in Galilee and ended up here!"

JESUS BROUGHT BEFORE HEROD

Now when Pilate heard this, he asked whether the man was a Galilean. When he learned that he was from Herod's jurisdiction, he sent him over to Herod, who also happened to be in Jerusalem at that time. When Herod saw Jesus, he was very glad, for he had long desired to see him because he had heard about him and was hoping to see him perform some miraculous sign. So Herod questioned him at considerable length; Jesus gave him no answer. The chief priests and the experts in the law were there, vehemently accusing him. Even Herod with his soldiers treated him with contempt and mocked him. Then, dressing him in elegant clothes, Herod sent him back to Pilate. That very day Herod and Pilate became friends with each other, for prior to this they had been enemies.

JESUS BROUGHT BEFORE THE CROWD

Then Pilate called together the chief priests, the leaders, and the people, and said to them, "You brought me this man as one who was misleading the people. When I examined him before you, I did not find this man guilty of anything you accused him of doing. Neither did Herod, for he sent him back to us. Look, he has done nothing deserving death. I will therefore have him flogged and release him."

But they all shouted out together, "Take this man away! Release Barabbas for us!" (This was a man who had been thrown into prison for an insurrection started in the city, and for murder.) Pilate addressed them once again because he wanted to release Jesus. But they kept on shouting, "Crucify, crucify him!"

A third time he said to them, "Why? What wrong has he done? I have found him guilty of no crime deserving death. I will therefore flog him and release him." But they were insistent, demanding with loud shouts that he be crucified. And their shouts prevailed. So Pilate decided that their demand should be granted. He released the man they asked for, who had been thrown in prison for insurrection and murder. But he handed Jesus over to their will.

THE CRUCIFIXION

As they led him away, they seized Simon of Cyrene, who was coming in from the country. They placed the cross on his back and made him carry it behind Jesus. A great number of the people followed him, among them women who were mourning and wailing for him. But Jesus turned to them and said, "Daughters of Jerusalem, do not weep for me, but weep for yourselves and for your children. For this is certain: The days are coming when they will say, 'Blessed are the barren, the wombs that never bore children, and the breasts that never nursed!' Then they will begin *to say to the mountains, 'Fall on us!' and to the hills, 'Cover us!'* For if such things are done when the wood is green, what will happen when it is dry?"

Two other criminals were also led away to be executed with him. So when they came to

the place that is called "The Skull," they crucified him there, along with the criminals, one
on his right and one on his left. [But Jesus said,
"Father, forgive them, for they don't know
what they are doing."] Then *they threw dice to
divide his clothes.* The people also stood there
watching, but the leaders ridiculed him, saying, "He saved others. Let him save himself if
he is the Christ of God, his chosen one!" The
soldiers also mocked him, coming up and offering him sour wine, and saying, "If you are
the king of the Jews, save yourself!" There was
also an inscription over him, "This is the king
of the Jews."

One of the criminals who was hanging
there railed at him, saying, "Aren't you the
Christ? Save yourself and us!" But the other
rebuked him, saying, "Don't you fear God,
since you are under the same sentence of
condemnation? And we rightly so, for we are
getting what we deserve for what we did, but
this man has done nothing wrong." Then he
said, "Jesus, remember me when you come in
your kingdom." And Jesus said to him, "I tell
you the truth, today you will be with me in
paradise."

It was now about noon, and darkness came
over the whole land until three in the afternoon, because the sun's light failed. The temple curtain was torn in two. Then Jesus, calling
out with a loud voice, said, "Father, *into your*

hands I commit my spirit!" And after he said this he breathed his last.

Now when the centurion saw what had happened, he praised God and said, "Certainly this man was innocent!" And all the crowds that had assembled for this spectacle, when they saw what had taken place, returned home beating their breasts. And all those who knew Jesus stood at a distance, and the women who had followed him from Galilee saw these things.

JESUS' BURIAL

Now there was a man named Joseph who was a member of the council, a good and righteous man. (He had not consented to their plan and action.) He was from the Judean town of Arimathea, and was looking forward to the kingdom of God. He went to Pilate and asked for the body of Jesus. Then he took it down, wrapped it in a linen cloth, and placed it in a tomb cut out of the rock, where no one had yet been buried. It was the day of preparation, and the Sabbath was beginning. The women who had accompanied Jesus from Galilee followed, and they saw the tomb and how his body was laid in it. Then they returned and prepared aromatic spices and perfumes.

On the Sabbath they rested according to the commandment.

CHAPTER 24

THE RESURRECTION

Now on the first day of the week, at early dawn, the women went to the tomb, taking the aromatic spices they had prepared. They found that the stone had been rolled away from the tomb, but when they went in, they did not find the body of the Lord Jesus. While they were perplexed about this, suddenly two men stood beside them in dazzling attire. The women were terribly frightened and bowed their faces to the ground, but the men said to them, "Why do you look for the living among the dead? He is not here, but has been raised! Remember how he told you, while he was still in Galilee, that the Son of Man must be delivered into the hands of sinful men, and be crucified, and on the third day rise again." Then the women remembered his words, and when they returned from the tomb, they told all these things to the eleven and to all the rest. Now it was Mary Magdalene, Joanna, Mary the mother of James, and the other women with them who told these things to the apostles. But these words seemed like pure nonsense to them, and they did not believe them. But Peter got up and ran to the tomb. He bent down and saw only the strips of linen cloth; then he went home, wondering what had happened.

JESUS WALKS THE ROAD TO EMMAUS

Now that very day two of them were on their way to a village called Emmaus, about seven miles from Jerusalem. They were talking to each other about all the things that had happened. While they were talking and debating these things, Jesus himself approached and began to accompany them (but their eyes were kept from recognizing him). Then he said to them, "What are these matters you are discussing so intently as you walk along?" And they stood still, looking sad. Then one of them, named Cleopas, answered him, "Are you the only visitor to Jerusalem who doesn't know the things that have happened there in these days?" He said to them, "What things?" "The things concerning Jesus the Nazarene," they replied, "a man who, with his powerful deeds and words, proved to be a prophet before God and all the people; and how our chief priests and leaders handed him over to be condemned to death, and crucified him. But we had hoped that he was the one who was going to redeem Israel. Not only this, but it is now the third day since these things happened. Furthermore, some women of our group amazed us. They were at the tomb early this morning, and when they did not find his body, they came back and said they had seen a vision of angels, who said he was alive. Then some of those who were with us went to the tomb and found it just as the women had said, but they did not see him." So he said to them, "You foolish people—how slow of heart to believe all that the prophets have spoken! Wasn't it necessary for the Christ to suffer these things and enter into his glory?" Then beginning with Moses and all the prophets, he interpreted to them the things written about himself in all the scriptures.

So they approached the village where they were going. He acted as though he wanted to go farther, but they urged him, "Stay with us because it is getting toward evening and the day is almost done." So he went in to stay with them.

When he had taken his place at the table with them, he took the bread, blessed and broke it, and gave it to them. At this point their eyes were opened and they recognized him. Then he vanished out of their sight. They said to each other, "Didn't our hearts burn within us while he was speaking with us on the road, while he was explaining the scriptures to us?" So they got up that very hour and returned to Jerusalem. They found the eleven and those with them gathered together and saying, "The Lord has really risen and has appeared to Simon!" Then they told what had happened on the road, and how they recognized him when he broke the bread.

JESUS MAKES A FINAL APPEARANCE

While they were saying these things, Jesus himself stood among them and said to them, "Peace be with you." But they were startled and terrified, thinking they saw a ghost. Then he said to them, "Why are you frightened, and why do doubts arise in your hearts? Look at my hands and my feet; it's me! Touch me and see; a ghost does not have flesh and bones like you see I have." When he had said this, he showed them his hands and his feet. And while they still could not believe it (because of their joy) and were amazed, he said to them, "Do you have anything here to eat?" So they gave him a piece of broiled fish, and he took it and ate it in front of them.

JESUS' FINAL COMMISSION

Then he said to them, "These are my words that I spoke to you while I was still with you, that everything written about me in the law of Moses and the prophets and the psalms must be fulfilled." Then he opened their minds so they could understand the scriptures, and said to them, "Thus it stands written that the Christ would suffer and would rise from the dead on the third day, and repentance for the forgiveness of sins would be proclaimed in his name to all nations, beginning from Jerusalem. You are witnesses of these things. And look, I am sending you what my Father promised. But stay in the city until you have been clothed with power from on high."

JESUS' DEPARTURE

Then Jesus led them out as far as Bethany, and lifting up his hands, he blessed them. Now during the blessing he departed and was taken up into heaven. So they worshiped him and returned to Jerusalem with great joy, and were continually in the temple courts blessing God.

ACTS

PROLOGUE

When Luke told Jesus' story, he had described Jesus' ministry and how he brought the news of salvation into the world. The story, however, was not over. Far from it. Jesus was no longer on earth, but his followers were. And Jesus had left them with a mission to fulfill. They were to continue what he had begun—they were to spread Jesus' message of forgiveness, love, and hope throughout the world. They would begin where they were at the time, in Jerusalem. Then they would move into the surrounding area of Judea. After that, they would cross into neighboring Samaria. And finally they would travel throughout the entire world.

In many ways, this geographical expansion of the church gets to the heart of the story Luke needed to tell. Jesus had changed everything. Because of Jesus, people are changed. Families are changed. Nations are changed. The life, death, and resurrection of Jesus sent shock waves of change throughout the world, waves that are still felt to this day.

CHAPTER 1

JESUS ASCENDS TO HEAVEN

I wrote the former account, Theophilus, about all that Jesus began to do and teach until the day he was taken up to heaven, after he had given orders by the Holy Spirit to the apostles he had chosen. To the same apostles also, after his suffering, he presented himself alive with many convincing proofs. He was seen by them over a forty-day period and spoke about matters concerning the kingdom of God. While he was with them, he declared, "Do not leave Jerusalem, but wait there for what my Father promised, which you heard about from me. For John baptized with water, but you will be baptized with the Holy Spirit not many days from now."

So when they had gathered together, they began to ask him, "Lord, is this the time when you are restoring the kingdom to Israel?" He told them, "You are not permitted to know the times or periods that the Father has set by his own authority. But you will receive power when the Holy Spirit has come upon you, and you will be my witnesses in Jerusalem, and in all Judea and Samaria, and to the farthest parts of the earth." After he had said this, while they were watching, he was lifted up and a cloud hid him from their sight. As they were still staring into the sky while he was going, suddenly two men in white clothing stood near them and said, "Men of Galilee, why do you stand here looking up into the sky? This same Jesus who has been taken up from you into heaven will come back in the same way you saw him go into heaven."

A REPLACEMENT FOR JUDAS IS CHOSEN

Then they returned to Jerusalem from the mountain called the Mount of Olives (which is near Jerusalem, a Sabbath day's journey away). When they had entered Jerusalem, they went to the upstairs room where they were staying. Peter and John, and James, and Andrew, Philip and Thomas, Bartholomew and Matthew, James son of Alphaeus and Simon the Zealot, and Judas son of James were there. All these continued together in prayer with one mind, together with the women, along with Mary the mother of Jesus, and his brothers. In those days Peter stood up among the believers (a gathering of about 120 people) and said, "Brothers, the scripture had to be fulfilled that the Holy Spirit foretold through David concerning Judas—who became the guide for those who arrested Jesus—for he was counted as one of us and received a share in this ministry." (Now this man Judas acquired a field with the reward of his unjust deed, and falling headfirst he burst open in the middle and all his intestines gushed out. This became known to all who lived in Jerusalem, so that in their own language they called that field *Hakeldama,* that is, "Field of Blood.") "For it is written in the book of Psalms, '*Let his house become deserted, and let there be no one to live in it,*' and '*Let another take his position of responsibility.*' Thus one of the men who have accompanied us during all the time the Lord Jesus associated with us, beginning from his baptism by John until the day he was taken up from us—one of these must become a witness of his resurrection together with us." So they proposed two candidates: Joseph called Barsabbas (also called Justus) and Matthias. Then they prayed, "Lord, you know the hearts of all. Show us which one of these two you have chosen to assume the task of this service and apostleship from which Judas turned aside to go to his own place." Then they cast lots for them, and the one chosen was Matthias; so he was counted with the eleven apostles.

CHAPTER 2

THE HOLY SPIRIT AND THE DAY OF PENTECOST

Now when the day of Pentecost had come, they were all together in one place. Suddenly a sound like a violent wind blowing came from heaven and filled the entire house where they were sitting. And tongues spreading out like a fire appeared to them and came to rest on each one of them. All of them were filled with the Holy Spirit, and they began to speak in other languages as the Spirit enabled them.

Now there were devout Jews from every nation under heaven residing in Jerusalem. When this sound occurred, a crowd gathered and was in confusion because each one heard them speaking in his own language. Completely baffled, they said, "Aren't all these who are speaking Galileans? And how is it that each one of us hears them in our own native language? Parthians, Medes, Elamites, and residents of Mesopotamia, Judea and Cappadocia, Pontus and the province of Asia, Phrygia and Pamphylia, Egypt and the parts of Libya near Cyrene, and visitors from Rome, both Jews and proselytes, Cretans and Arabs—we hear them speaking in our own languages about the great deeds God has done!" All were astounded and greatly confused, saying to one another, "What does this mean?" But others jeered at the speakers, saying, "They are drunk on new wine!"

PETER'S ADDRESS ON THE DAY OF PENTECOST

But Peter stood up with the eleven, raised his voice, and addressed them: "You men of Judea and all you who live in Jerusalem, know this and listen carefully to what I say. In spite of what you think, these men are not drunk, for it is only nine o'clock in the morning. But this is what was spoken about through the prophet Joel:

'*And* in the last days *it will be*,' *God says*,
'*that I will pour out my Spirit on all
     people,*
*and your sons and your daughters will
     prophesy,*
and your young men will see visions,
and your old men will dream dreams.
*Even on my servants, both men and
     women,*
*I will pour out my Spirit in those days, and
     they will prophesy.*
*And I will perform wonders in the sky
     above*
and miraculous signs on the earth below,
blood and fire and clouds of smoke.
The sun will be changed to darkness
and the moon to blood
*before the great and glorious day of the
     Lord comes.*
*And then everyone who calls on the name
     of the Lord will be saved.*'

"Men of Israel, listen to these words: Jesus the Nazarene, a man clearly attested to you by God with powerful deeds, wonders, and miraculous signs that God performed among you through him, just as you yourselves know—this man, who was handed over by the predetermined plan and foreknowledge of God, you executed by nailing him to a cross at the hands of Gentiles. But God raised him up, having released him from the pains of death because it was not possible for him to be held in its power. For David says about him,

'I saw the Lord always in front of me,
for he is at my right hand so that I will not
be shaken.
Therefore my heart was glad and my
tongue rejoiced;
my body also will live in hope,
because you will not leave my soul in
Hades,
nor permit your Holy One to experience
decay.
You have made known to me the paths of
life;
you will make me full of joy with your
presence.'

"Brothers, I can speak confidently to you about our forefather David, that he both died and was buried, and his tomb is with us to this day. So then, because he was a prophet and knew that God *had sworn to him with an oath to seat one of his descendants on his throne,* David by foreseeing this spoke about the resurrection of the Christ, that *he was neither abandoned to Hades,* nor did his body *experience decay.* This Jesus God raised up, and we are all witnesses of it. So then, exalted to the right hand of God, and having received the promise of the Holy Spirit from the Father, he has poured out what you both see and hear. For David did not ascend into heaven, but he himself says,

> 'The Lord said to my lord,
> "Sit at my right hand
> until I make your enemies a footstool for
>   your feet."'

Therefore let all the house of Israel know beyond a doubt that God has made this Jesus whom you crucified both Lord and Christ."

THE RESPONSE TO PETER'S ADDRESS

Now when they heard this, they were acutely distressed and said to Peter and the rest of the apostles, "What should we do, brothers?" Peter said to them, "Repent, and each one of you be baptized in the name of Jesus Christ for the forgiveness of your sins, and you will receive the gift of the Holy Spirit. For the promise is for you and your children, and for all who are far away, as many as the Lord our God will call to himself." With many other words he testified and exhorted them saying, "Save yourselves from this perverse generation!" So those who accepted his message were baptized, and that day about 3,000 people were added.

THE FELLOWSHIP OF THE EARLY BELIEVERS

They were devoting themselves to the apostles' teaching and to fellowship, to the breaking of bread and to prayer. Reverential awe came over everyone, and many wonders and miraculous signs came about by the apostles.

All who believed were together and held everything in common, and they began selling their property and possessions and distributing the proceeds to everyone, as anyone had need. Every day they continued to gather together by common consent in the temple courts, breaking bread from house to house, sharing their food with glad and humble hearts, praising God and having the good will of all the people. And the Lord was adding to their number every day those who were being saved.

CHAPTER 3

PETER AND JOHN HEAL A LAME MAN AT THE TEMPLE

Now Peter and John were going up to the temple at the time for prayer, at three o'clock in the afternoon. And a man lame from birth was being carried up, who was placed at the temple gate called "the Beautiful Gate" every day so he could beg for money from those going into the temple courts. When he saw Peter and John about to go into the temple courts, he asked them for money. Peter looked directly at him (as did John) and said, "Look at us!" So the lame man paid attention to them, expecting to receive something from them. But Peter said, "I have no silver or gold, but what I do have I give you. In the name of Jesus Christ the Nazarene, stand up and walk!" Then Peter took hold of him by the right hand and raised him up, and at once the man's feet and ankles were made strong. He jumped up, stood and began walking around, and he entered the temple courts with them, walking and leaping and praising God. All the people saw him walking and praising God, and they recognized him as the man who used to sit and ask for donations at the Beautiful Gate of the temple, and they were filled with astonishment and amazement at what had happened to him.

PETER ADDRESSES THE CROWD

While the man was hanging on to Peter and John, all the people, completely astounded, ran together to them in the covered walkway called Solomon's Portico. When Peter saw this, he declared to the people, "Men of Israel, why are you amazed at this? Why do you stare at us as if we had made this man walk by our own power or piety? The God of Abraham, Isaac, and Jacob, the God of our forefathers, has glorified his servant Jesus, whom you handed over and rejected in the presence of Pilate after he had decided to release him. But you rejected the Holy and Righteous One and asked that a man who was a murderer be released to you. You killed the Originator of life, whom God raised from the dead. To this fact we are witnesses! And on the basis of faith in Jesus' name, his very name has made this man—whom you see and know—strong. The faith that is through Jesus has given him this complete health in the presence of you all. And now, brothers, I know you acted in ignorance, as your rulers did too. But the things God foretold long ago through all the prophets—that his Christ would suffer—he has fulfilled in this way. Therefore repent and turn back so that your sins may be wiped out, so that times of refreshing may come from the presence of the Lord, and so that he may send the Messiah appointed for you—that is, Jesus. This one heaven must receive until the time all things are restored, which God declared from times long ago through his holy prophets. Moses said, *'The Lord your God will raise up for you a prophet like me from among your brothers. You must obey him in everything he tells you. Every person who does not obey that prophet will be destroyed and thus removed from the people.'* And all the prophets, from Samuel and those who followed him, have spoken about and announced these days. You are the sons of the prophets and of the covenant that God made with your ancestors, saying to Abraham, *'And in your descendants all the nations of the earth will be blessed.'* God raised up his servant and sent him first to you, to bless you by turning each one of you from your iniquities."

CHAPTER 4

THE ARREST AND TRIAL OF PETER AND JOHN

While Peter and John were speaking to the people, the priests and the commander of the temple guard and the Sadducees came up to them, angry because they were teaching the people and announcing in Jesus the resurrection of the dead. So they seized them and put them in jail until the next day (for it was already evening). But many of those who had listened to the message believed, and the number of the men came to about 5,000.

On the next day, their rulers, elders, and experts in the law came together in Jerusalem. Annas the high priest was there, and Caiaphas, John, Alexander, and others who were members of the high priest's family. After making Peter and John stand in their midst, they began to inquire, "By what power or by what name did you do this?" Then Peter, filled with the Holy Spirit, replied, "Rulers of the people and elders, if we are being examined today for a good deed done to a sick man—by what means this man was healed—let it be known to all of you and to all the people of Israel that by the name of Jesus Christ the Nazarene whom you crucified, whom God raised from the dead, this man stands before you healthy. This Jesus is *the stone that was rejected by* you, *the builders, that has become the cornerstone.* And there is salvation in no one else, for there is no other name under heaven given among people by which we must be saved."

When they saw the boldness of Peter and John, and discovered that they were uneducated and ordinary men, they were amazed and recognized these men had been with Jesus. And because they saw the man who had been healed standing with them, they had nothing to say against this. But when they had ordered them to go outside the council, they began to confer with one another, saying, "What should we do with these men? For it is plain to all who live in Jerusalem that a notable miraculous sign has come about through them, and we cannot deny it. But to keep this matter from spreading any further among the people, let us warn them to speak no more to anyone in this name." And they called them in and ordered them not to speak or teach at all in the name of Jesus. But Peter and John replied, "Whether it is right before God to obey you rather than God, you decide, for it is impossible for us not to speak about what we have seen and heard." After threatening them further, they released them, for they could not find how to punish them on account of the people, because they were all praising God for what had happened. For the man, on whom this miraculous sign of healing had been performed, was over forty years old.

THE FOLLOWERS OF JESUS
PRAY FOR BOLDNESS

When they were released, Peter and John went to their fellow believers and reported everything the high priests and the elders had said to them. When they heard this, they raised their voices to God with one mind and said, "Master of all, you who made the heaven, the earth, the sea, and everything that is in them, who said by the Holy Spirit through your servant David our forefather,

> *'Why do the nations rage,*
> *and the peoples plot foolish things?*
> *The kings of the earth stood together,*
> *and the rulers assembled together,*
> *against the Lord and against his Christ.'*

"For indeed both Herod and Pontius Pilate, with the Gentiles and the people of Israel, assembled together in this city against your holy servant Jesus, whom you anointed, to do as much as your power and your plan had decided beforehand would happen. And now, Lord, pay attention to their threats, and grant to your servants to speak your message with great courage, while you extend your hand to heal, and to bring about miraculous signs and wonders through the name of your holy servant Jesus." When they had prayed, the place where they were assembled together was shaken, and they were all filled with the Holy Spirit and began to speak the word of God courageously.

CONDITIONS AMONG THE EARLY BELIEVERS

The group of those who believed were of one heart and mind, and no one said that any of his possessions was his own, but everything was held in common. With great power the apostles were giving testimony to the resurrection of the Lord Jesus, and great grace was on them all. For there was no one needy among them because those who were owners of land or houses were selling them and bringing the proceeds from the sales and placing them at the apostles' feet. The proceeds were distributed to each, as anyone had need. So Joseph, a Levite who was a native of Cyprus, called by the apostles Barnabas (which is translated "son of encouragement"), sold a field that belonged to him and brought the money and placed it at the apostles' feet.

CHAPTER 5

THE JUDGMENT ON ANANIAS AND SAPPHIRA

Now a man named Ananias, together with Sapphira his wife, sold a piece of property. He kept back for himself part of the proceeds with his wife's knowledge; he brought only part of it and placed it at the apostles' feet. But Peter said, "Ananias, why has Satan filled your heart to lie to the Holy Spirit and keep back for yourself part of the proceeds from the sale of the land? Before it was sold, did it not belong to you? And when it was sold, was the money not at your disposal? How have you thought up this deed in your heart? You have not lied to people but to God!"

When Ananias heard these words he collapsed and died, and great fear gripped all who heard about it. So the young men came, wrapped him up, carried him out, and buried him. After an interval of about three hours, his wife came in, but she did not know what had happened. Peter said to her, "Tell me, were the two of you paid this amount for the land?" Sapphira said, "Yes, that much." Peter then told her, "Why have you agreed together to test the Spirit of the Lord? Look! The feet of those who have buried your husband are at the door, and they will carry you out!" At once she collapsed at his feet and died. So when the young men came in, they found her dead, and they carried her out and buried her beside her husband. Great fear gripped the whole church and all who heard about these things.

THE APOSTLES PERFORM MIRACULOUS SIGNS AND WONDERS

Now many miraculous signs and wonders came about among the people through the hands of the apostles. By common consent they were all meeting together in Solomon's Portico. None of the rest dared to join them, but the people held them in high honor. More and more believers in the Lord were added to their number, crowds of both men and women. Thus they even carried the sick out into the streets and put them on cots and pallets, so that when Peter came by at least his shadow would fall on some of them. A crowd of people from the towns around Jerusalem also came together, bringing the sick and those troubled by unclean spirits. They were all being healed.

FURTHER TROUBLE FOR THE APOSTLES

Now the high priest rose up, and all those with him (that is, the religious party of the Sadducees), and they were filled with jealousy. They laid hands on the apostles and put them in a public jail. But during the night an angel of the Lord opened the doors of the prison, led them out, and said, "Go and stand in the temple courts and proclaim to the people all the words of this life." When they heard this, they entered the temple courts at daybreak and began teaching.

Now when the high priest and those who were with him arrived, they summoned the Sanhedrin—that is, the whole high council of the Israelites—and sent to the jail to have the apostles brought before them. But the officers who came for them did not find them in the prison, so they returned and reported, "We found the jail locked securely and the guards standing at the doors, but when we opened them, we found no one inside." Now when the commander of the temple guard and the chief priests heard this report, they were greatly puzzled concerning it, wondering what this could be. But someone came and reported to them, "Look! The men you put in prison are standing in the temple courts and teaching the people!" Then the commander of the temple guard went with the officers and brought the apostles without the use of force (for they were afraid of being stoned by the people).

When they had brought them, they stood them before the council, and the high priest questioned them, saying, "We gave you strict orders not to teach in this name. Look, you have filled Jerusalem with your teaching, and you intend to bring this man's blood on us!" But Peter and the apostles replied, "We must obey God rather than people. The God of our forefathers raised up Jesus, whom you seized and killed by hanging him on a tree. God exalted him to his right hand as Leader and Savior, to give repentance to Israel and forgiveness of sins. And we are witnesses of these events, and so is the Holy Spirit whom God has given to those who obey him."

Now when they heard this, they became furious and wanted to execute them. But a Pharisee whose name was Gamaliel, a teacher of the law who was respected by all the people, stood up in the council and ordered the men to be put outside for a short time. Then he said to the council, "Men of Israel, pay close attention to what you are about to do to these men. For sometime ago Theudas rose up, claiming to be somebody, and about 400 men joined him. He was killed, and all who followed him were dispersed and nothing came of it. After him Judas the Galilean arose in the days of the census and incited people to follow him in revolt. He too was killed, and all who followed him were scattered. So in this case I say to you, stay away from these men and leave them alone because if this plan or this undertaking originates with people, it will come to nothing, but if it is from God, you will not be able to stop them, or you may even be found fighting against God." He convinced them, and they summoned the apostles and had them beaten. Then they ordered them not to speak in the name of Jesus and released them. So they left the council rejoicing because they had been considered worthy to suffer dishonor for the sake of the name. And every day both in the temple courts and from house to house, they did not stop teaching and proclaiming the good news that Jesus was the Christ.

CHAPTER 6

THE APPOINTMENT OF THE FIRST SEVEN DEACONS

Now in those days, when the disciples were growing in number, a complaint arose on the part of the Greek-speaking Jews against the native Hebraic Jews because their widows were being overlooked in the daily distribution of food. So the twelve called the whole group of the disciples together and said, "It is not right for us to neglect the word of God to wait on tables. But carefully select from among you, brothers, seven men who are well-attested, full of the Spirit and of wisdom, whom we may put in charge of this necessary task. But we will devote ourselves to prayer and to the ministry of the word." The proposal pleased the entire group, so they chose Stephen, a man full of faith and of the Holy Spirit, with Philip, Prochorus, Nicanor, Timon, Parmenas, and Nicolas, a Gentile convert to Judaism from Antioch. They stood these men before the apostles, who prayed and placed their hands on them. The word of God continued to spread, the number of disciples in Jerusalem increased greatly, and a large group of priests became obedient to the faith.

STEPHEN IS ARRESTED

Now Stephen, full of grace and power, was performing great wonders and miraculous signs among the people. But some men from the Synagogue of the Freedmen (as it was called), both Cyrenians and Alexandrians, as well as some from Cilicia and the province of Asia, stood up and argued with Stephen. Yet they were not able to resist the wisdom and the Spirit with which he spoke. Then they secretly instigated some men to say, "We have heard this man speaking blasphemous words against Moses and God." They incited the people, the elders, and the experts in the law; then they approached Stephen, seized him, and brought him before the council. They brought forward false witnesses who said, "This man does not stop saying things against this holy place and the law. For we have heard him saying that Jesus the Nazarene will destroy this place and change the customs that Moses handed down to us." All who were sitting in the council looked intently at Stephen and saw his face was like the face of an angel.

CHAPTER 7

STEPHEN'S DEFENSE BEFORE THE COUNCIL

Then the high priest said, "Are these things true?" So he replied, "Brothers and fathers, listen to me. The God of glory appeared to our forefather Abraham when he was in Mesopotamia, before he settled in Haran, and said to him, '*Go out from your country and from your relatives, and come to the land I will show you.*' Then he went out from the country of the Chaldeans and settled in Haran. After his father died, God made him move to this country where you now live. He did not give any of it to him for an inheritance, not even a foot of ground, yet God promised *to give it to him as his possession, and to his descendants after him,* even though Abraham as yet had no child. But God spoke as follows: 'Your *descendants will be foreigners in a foreign country, whose citizens will enslave them and mistreat them for 400 years. But I will punish the nation they serve as slaves,'* said God, *'and after these things they will come out of there* and *worship me in this place.'* Then God gave Abraham the covenant of circumcision, and so he became the father of Isaac and circumcised him when he was eight days old, and Isaac became the father of Jacob, and Jacob of the 12 patriarchs. The patriarchs, because they were jealous of Joseph, sold him into Egypt. But God was with him, and rescued him from all his troubles, and granted him favor and wisdom in the presence of Pharaoh, king of Egypt, who made him ruler over Egypt and over all his household. Then a famine occurred throughout Egypt and Canaan, causing great suffering, and our ancestors could not find food. So when Jacob heard that there was grain in Egypt, he sent our ancestors there the first time. On their second visit Joseph made himself known to his brothers again, and Joseph's family became known to Pharaoh. So Joseph sent a message and invited his father Jacob and all his relatives to come, seventy-five people in all. So Jacob went down to Egypt and died there, along with our ancestors, and their bones were later moved to Shechem and placed in the tomb that Abraham had bought for a certain sum of money from the sons of Hamor in Shechem.

"But as the time drew near for God to fulfill the promise he had declared to Abraham, the people increased greatly in number in Egypt, until *another king who did not know about Joseph ruled over Egypt.* This was the one who exploited our people and was cruel to our ancestors, forcing them to abandon their infants so they would die. At that time Moses was born, and he was beautiful to God. For three months he was brought up in his father's house, and when he had been abandoned, Pharaoh's daughter adopted him and brought him up as her own son. So Moses was trained in all the wisdom of the Egyptians and was powerful in his words and deeds. But when he was about forty years old, it entered his mind to visit his fellow countrymen the Israelites. When he saw one of them being hurt unfairly, Moses came to his defense and avenged the person who was mistreated by striking down the Egyptian. He thought his own people would understand that God was delivering them through him, but they did not understand. The next day Moses saw two men fighting and tried to make peace between them, saying, 'Men, you are brothers; why are you hurting one another?' But the man who was unfairly hurting his neighbor pushed Moses aside, saying,

'*Who made you a ruler and judge over us? You don't want to kill me the way you killed the Egyptian yesterday, do you?*' When the man said this, Moses fled and became a foreigner in the land of Midian, where he became the father of two sons.

"After forty years had passed, *an angel appeared to him in the desert of Mount Sinai, in the flame of a burning bush.* When Moses saw it, he was amazed at the sight, and when he approached to investigate, there came the voice of the Lord, '*I am the God of your forefathers, the God of Abraham, Isaac, and Jacob.*' Moses began to tremble and did not dare to look more closely. *But the Lord said to him, 'Take the sandals off your feet, for the place where you are standing is holy ground. I have certainly seen the suffering of my people who are in Egypt and have heard their groaning, and I have come down to rescue them. Now come, I will send you to Egypt.*' This same Moses they had rejected, saying, '*Who made you a ruler and judge?*' God sent as both ruler and deliverer through the hand of the angel who appeared to him in the bush. This man led them out, performing wonders and miraculous signs in the land of Egypt, at the Red Sea, and in the wilderness for forty years. This is the Moses who said to the Israelites, '*God will raise up for you a prophet like me from among your brothers.*' This is the man who was in the congregation in the wilderness with the angel who spoke to him at Mount Sinai, and with our ancestors, and he received living oracles to give to you. Our ancestors were unwilling to obey him, but pushed him aside and turned back to Egypt in their hearts, saying to Aaron, '*Make us gods who will go in front of us, for this Moses, who led us out of the land of Egypt —we do not know what has happened to him!*' At that time they made an idol in the form of a calf, brought a sacrifice to the idol, and began rejoicing in the works of their hands. But God turned away from them and gave them over to worship the host of heaven, as it is written in the book of the prophets: '*It was not to me that you offered slain animals and sacrifices forty years in the wilderness, was it, house of Israel? But you took along the tabernacle of Moloch and the star of the god Rephan, the images you made to worship, but I will deport you beyond Babylon.*' Our ancestors had the tabernacle of testimony in the wilderness, just as God who spoke to Moses ordered him to make it according to the design he had seen. Our ancestors received possession of it and brought it in with Joshua when they dispossessed the nations that God drove out before our ancestors, until the time of David. He found favor with God and asked that he could find a dwelling place for the house of Jacob. But Solomon built a house for him. Yet the Most High does not live in houses made by human hands, as the prophet says,

'Heaven is my throne,
and earth is the footstool for my feet.
What kind of house will you build for me,
*   says the Lord,*
or what is my resting place?
Did my hand not make all these things?'

"You stubborn people, with uncircumcised hearts and ears! You are always resisting the Holy Spirit, like your ancestors did! Which of the prophets did your ancestors not persecute? They killed those who foretold long ago the coming of the Righteous One, whose betrayers and murderers you have now become! You received the law by decrees given by angels, but you did not obey it."

STEPHEN IS KILLED

When they heard these things, they became furious and ground their teeth at him. But Stephen, full of the Holy Spirit, looked intently toward heaven and saw the glory of God, and Jesus standing at the right hand of God. "Look!" he said. "I see the heavens opened, and the Son of Man standing at the right hand of God!" But they covered their ears, shouting out with a loud voice, and rushed at him with one intent. When they had driven him out of the city, they began to stone him, and the witnesses laid their cloaks at the feet of a young man named Saul. They continued to stone Stephen while he prayed, "Lord Jesus, receive my spirit!" Then he fell to his knees and cried out with a loud voice, "Lord, do not hold this sin against them!" When he had said this, he died.

CHAPTER 8

And Saul agreed completely with killing him.

SAUL BEGINS TO PERSECUTE THE CHURCH

Now on that day a great persecution began against the church in Jerusalem, and all except the apostles were forced to scatter throughout the regions of Judea and Samaria. Some devout men buried Stephen and made loud lamentation over him. But Saul was trying to destroy the church; entering one house after another, he dragged off both men and women and put them in prison.

PHILIP PREACHES IN SAMARIA

Now those who had been forced to scatter went around proclaiming the good news of the word. Philip went down to the main city of Samaria and began proclaiming the Christ to them. The crowds were paying attention with one mind to what Philip said, as they heard and saw the miraculous signs he was performing. For unclean spirits, crying with loud shrieks, were coming out of many who were possessed, and many paralyzed and lame people were healed. So there was great joy in that city.

Now in that city was a man named Simon, who had been practicing magic and amazing the people of Samaria, claiming to be someone great. All the people, from the least to the greatest, paid close attention to him, saying, "This man is the power of God that is called 'Great.' " And they paid close attention to him because he had amazed them for a long time with his magic. But when they believed Philip as he was proclaiming the good news about the kingdom of God and the name of Jesus Christ, they began to be baptized, both men and women. Even Simon himself believed, and after he was baptized, he stayed close to Philip constantly, and when he saw the signs and great miracles that were occurring, he was amazed.

Now when the apostles in Jerusalem heard that Samaria had accepted the word of God, they sent Peter and John to them. These two went down and prayed for them so that they would receive the Holy Spirit. (For the Spirit had not yet come upon any of them, but they had only been baptized in the name of the Lord Jesus.) Then Peter and John placed their hands on the Samaritans, and they received the Holy Spirit.

Now Simon, when he saw that the Spirit was given through the laying on of the apostles' hands, offered them money, saying, "Give me this power too, so that everyone I place my hands on may receive the Holy Spirit." But Peter said to him, "May your silver perish with you because you thought you could acquire God's gift with money! You have no share or part in this matter because your heart is not right before God! Therefore repent of this wickedness of yours, and pray to the Lord that he may perhaps forgive you for the intent of your heart. For I see that you are bitterly envious and in bondage to sin." But Simon replied, "You pray to the Lord for me so that nothing of what you have said may happen to me."

So after Peter and John had solemnly testified and spoken the word of the Lord, they started back to Jerusalem, proclaiming the good news to many Samaritan villages as they went.

PHILIP AND THE ETHIOPIAN EUNUCH

Then an angel of the Lord said to Philip, "Get up and go south on the road that goes down from Jerusalem to Gaza." (This is a desert road.) So he got up and went. There he met an Ethiopian eunuch, a court official of Candace, queen of the Ethiopians, who was in charge of all her treasury. He had come to Jerusalem to worship, and was returning home, sitting in his chariot, reading the prophet Isaiah. Then the Spirit said to Philip, "Go over and join this chariot." So Philip ran up to it and heard the man reading the prophet Isaiah. He asked him, "Do you understand what you're reading?" The man replied, "How in the world can I, unless someone guides me?" So he invited Philip to come up and sit with him. Now the passage of scripture the man was reading was this:

"He was led like a sheep to slaughter,
and like a lamb before its shearer
is silent,
so he did not open his mouth.
In humiliation justice was taken
from him.
Who can describe his posterity?
For his life was taken away from the
earth."

Then the eunuch said to Philip, "Please tell me, who is the prophet saying this about— himself or someone else?" So Philip started speaking, and beginning with this scripture proclaimed the good news about Jesus to him. Now as they were going along the road, they came to some water, and the eunuch said, "Look, there is water! What is to stop me from being baptized?" So he ordered the chariot to stop, and both Philip and the eunuch went down into the water, and Philip baptized him. Now when they came up out of the water, the Spirit of the Lord snatched Philip away, and the eunuch did not see him any more, but went on his way rejoicing. Philip, however, found himself at Azotus, and as he passed through the area, he proclaimed the good news to all the towns until he came to Caesarea.

CHAPTER 9

THE CONVERSION OF SAUL

Meanwhile Saul, still breathing out threats to murder the Lord's disciples, went to the high priest and requested letters from him to the synagogues in Damascus, so that if he found any who belonged to the Way, either men or women, he could bring them as prisoners to Jerusalem. As he was going along, approaching Damascus, suddenly a light from heaven flashed around him. He fell to the ground and heard a voice saying to him, "Saul, Saul, why are you persecuting me?" So he said, "Who are you, Lord?" He replied, "I am Jesus whom you are persecuting! But stand up and enter the city, and you will be told what you must do." (Now the men who were traveling with him stood there speechless because they heard the voice but saw no one.) So Saul got up from the ground, but although his eyes were open, he could see nothing. Leading him by the hand, his companions brought him into Damascus. For three days he could not see, and he neither ate nor drank anything.

Now there was a disciple in Damascus named Ananias. The Lord said to him in a vision, "Ananias," and he replied, "Here I am,

Lord." Then the Lord told him, "Get up and go to the street called 'Straight,' and at Judas' house look for a man from Tarsus named Saul. For he is praying, and he has seen in a vision a man named Ananias come in and place his hands on him so that he may see again." But Ananias replied, "Lord, I have heard from many people about this man, how much harm he has done to your saints in Jerusalem, and here he has authority from the chief priests to imprison all who call on your name!" But the Lord said to him, "Go, because this man is my chosen instrument to carry my name before Gentiles and kings and the people of Israel. For I will show him how much he must suffer for the sake of my name." So Ananias departed and entered the house, placed his hands on Saul and said, "Brother Saul, the Lord Jesus, who appeared to you on the road as you came here, has sent me so that you may see again and be filled with the Holy Spirit." Immediately something like scales fell from his eyes, and he could see again. He got up and was baptized, and after taking some food, his strength returned.

For several days he was with the disciples in Damascus, and immediately he began to proclaim Jesus in the synagogues, saying, "This man is the Son of God." All who heard him were amazed and were saying, "Is this not the man who in Jerusalem was ravaging those who call on this name, and who had come here to bring them as prisoners to the chief priests?" But Saul became more and more capable, and was causing consternation among the Jews who lived in Damascus by proving that Jesus is the Christ.

SAUL'S ESCAPE FROM DAMASCUS

Now after some days had passed, the Jews plotted together to kill him, but Saul learned of their plot against him. They were also watching the city gates day and night so that they could kill him. But his disciples took him at night and let him down through an opening in the wall by lowering him in a basket.

SAUL RETURNS TO JERUSALEM

When he arrived in Jerusalem, he attempted to associate with the disciples, and they were all afraid of him because they did not believe that he was a disciple. But Barnabas took Saul, brought him to the apostles, and related to them how he had seen the Lord on the road, that the Lord had spoken to him, and how in Damascus he had spoken out boldly in the name of Jesus. So he was staying with them, associating openly with them in Jerusalem, speaking out boldly in the name of the Lord. He was speaking and debating with the Greek-speaking Jews, but they were trying to kill him. When the brothers found out about this, they brought him down to Caesarea and sent him away to Tarsus.

Then the church throughout Judea, Galilee,

and Samaria experienced peace and thus was strengthened. Living in the fear of the Lord and in the encouragement of the Holy Spirit, the church increased in numbers.

PETER HEALS AENEAS

Now as Peter was traveling around from place to place, he also came down to the saints who lived in Lydda. He found there a man named Aeneas who had been confined to a mattress for eight years because he was paralyzed. Peter said to him, "Aeneas, Jesus the Christ heals you. Get up and make your own bed!" And immediately he got up. All those who lived in Lydda and Sharon saw him, and they turned to the Lord.

PETER RAISES DORCAS

Now in Joppa there was a disciple named Tabitha (which in translation means Dorcas). She was continually doing good deeds and acts of charity. At that time she became sick and died. When they had washed her body, they placed it in an upstairs room. Because Lydda was near Joppa, when the disciples heard that Peter was there, they sent two men to him and urged him, "Come to us without delay." So Peter got up and went with them, and when he arrived they brought him to the upper room. All the widows stood beside him, crying and showing him the tunics and other clothing Dorcas used to make while she was with them. But Peter sent them all outside, knelt down, and prayed. Turning to the body, he said, "Tabitha, get up." Then she opened her eyes, and when she saw Peter, she sat up. He gave her his hand and helped her get up. Then he called the saints and widows and presented her alive. This became known throughout all Joppa, and many believed in the Lord. So Peter stayed many days in Joppa with a man named Simon, a tanner.

CHAPTER 10

PETER VISITS CORNELIUS

Now there was a man in Caesarea named Cornelius, a centurion of what was known as the Italian Cohort. He was a devout, God-fearing man, as was all his household; he did many acts of charity for the people and prayed to God regularly. About three o'clock one afternoon he saw clearly in a vision an angel of God who came in and said to him, "Cornelius." Staring at him and becoming greatly afraid, Cornelius replied, "What is it, Lord?" The angel said to him, "Your prayers and your acts of charity have gone up as a memorial before God. Now send men to Joppa and summon a man named Simon, who is called Peter. This man is staying as a guest with a man named Simon, a tanner, whose house is by the sea." When the angel who had spoken to him departed, Cornelius called two of his personal servants and a devout soldier from among those who served him, and when he had explained everything to them, he sent them to Joppa.

About noon the next day, while they were on their way and approaching the city, Peter went up on the roof to pray. He became hungry and wanted to eat, but while they were preparing the meal, a trance came over him. He saw heaven opened and an object something like a large sheet descending, being let down to earth by its four corners. In it were all kinds of four-footed animals and reptiles of the earth and wild birds. Then a voice said to him, "Get up, Peter; slaughter and eat!" But Peter said, "Certainly not, Lord, for I have never eaten anything defiled and ritually unclean!" The voice spoke to him again, a second time, "What God has made clean, you must not consider ritually unclean!" This happened three times, and immediately the object was taken up into heaven.

Now while Peter was puzzling over what the vision he had seen could signify, the men sent by Cornelius had learned where Simon's house was and approached the gate. They called out to ask if Simon, known as Peter, was staying there as a guest. While Peter was still thinking seriously about the vision, the Spirit said to him, "Look! Three men are looking for you. But get up, go down, and accompany them without hesitation because I have sent them." So Peter went down to the men and said, "Here I am, the person you're looking for. Why have you come?" They said, "Cornelius the centurion, a righteous and God-fearing man, well spoken of by the whole Jewish nation, was directed by a holy angel to summon you to his house and to hear a message from you." So Peter invited them in and entertained them as guests.

On the next day he got up and set out with them, and some of the brothers from Joppa accompanied him. The following day he entered Caesarea. Now Cornelius was waiting anxiously for them and had called together his relatives and close friends. So when Peter came in, Cornelius met him, fell at his feet, and worshiped him. But Peter helped him up, saying, "Stand up. I too am a mere mortal." Peter continued talking with him as he went in, and he found many people gathered together. He said to them, "You know that it is unlawful for a Jew to associate with or visit a Gentile, yet God has shown me that I should call no person defiled or ritually unclean. Therefore when you sent for me, I came without any objection. Now may I ask why you sent for me?" Cornelius replied, "Four days ago at this very hour, at three o'clock in the afternoon, I was praying in my house, and suddenly a man in shining clothing stood before me and said, 'Cornelius, your prayer has been heard and your acts of charity have been remembered before God. Therefore send to Joppa and summon Simon, who is called Peter. This man is staying as a guest in the house of Simon the tanner, by the sea.' Therefore I sent for you at once, and you were kind enough to come. So now we are all here in the presence of God to listen to everything the Lord has commanded you to say to us."

Then Peter started speaking: "I now truly understand that God does not show favoritism in dealing with people, but in every nation the person who fears him and does what is right is welcomed before him. You know the message he sent to the people of Israel, proclaiming the good news of peace through Jesus Christ (he is Lord of all)—you know what happened throughout Judea, beginning from Galilee after the baptism that John announced: with respect to Jesus from Nazareth, that God anointed him with the Holy Spirit and with power. He went around doing good and healing all who were oppressed by the devil because God was with him. We are witnesses of all the things he did both in Judea and in Jerusalem. They killed him by hanging him on a tree, but God raised him up on the third day and caused him to be seen, not by all the people, but by us, the witnesses God had already chosen, who ate and drank with him after he rose from the dead. He commanded us to preach to the people and to warn them that he is the one appointed by God as judge of the living and the dead.

About him all the prophets testify, that everyone who believes in him receives forgiveness of sins through his name."

THE GENTILES RECEIVE THE HOLY SPIRIT

While Peter was still speaking these words, the Holy Spirit fell on all those who heard the message. The circumcised believers who had accompanied Peter were greatly astonished that the gift of the Holy Spirit had been poured out even on the Gentiles, for they heard them speaking in tongues and praising God. Then Peter said, "No one can withhold the water for these people to be baptized, who have received the Holy Spirit just as we did, can he?" So he gave orders to have them baptized in the name of Jesus Christ. Then they asked him to stay for several days.

CHAPTER 11

PETER DEFENDS HIS ACTIONS
TO THE JERUSALEM CHURCH

Now the apostles and the brothers who were throughout Judea heard that the Gentiles too had accepted the word of God. So when Peter went up to Jerusalem, the circumcised believers took issue with him, saying, "You went to uncircumcised men and shared a meal with them." But Peter began and explained it to them point by point, saying, "I was in the city of Joppa praying, and in a trance I saw a vision, an object something like a large sheet descending, being let down from heaven by its four corners, and it came to me. As I stared I looked into it and saw four-footed animals of the earth, wild animals, reptiles, and wild birds. I also heard a voice saying to me, 'Get up, Peter; slaughter and eat!' But I said, 'Certainly not, Lord, for nothing defiled or ritually unclean has ever entered my mouth!' But the voice replied a second time from heaven, 'What God has made clean, you must not consider ritually unclean!' This happened three times, and then everything was pulled up to heaven again. At that very moment, three men sent to me from Caesarea approached the house where we were staying. The Spirit told me to accompany them without hesitation. These six brothers also went with me, and we entered the man's house. He informed us how he had seen an angel standing in his house and saying, 'Send to Joppa and summon Simon, who is called Peter, who will speak a message to you by which you and your entire household will be saved.' Then as I began to speak, the Holy Spirit fell on them just as he did on us at the beginning. And I remembered the word of the Lord, as he used to say, 'John baptized with water, but you will be baptized with the Holy Spirit.' Therefore if God gave them the same gift as he also gave us after believing in the Lord Jesus Christ, who was I to hinder God?" When they heard this, they ceased their objections and praised God, saying, "So then, God has granted the repentance that leads to life even to the Gentiles."

ACTIVITY IN THE CHURCH AT ANTIOCH

Now those who had been scattered because of the persecution that took place over Stephen went as far as Phoenicia, Cyprus, and Antioch, speaking the message to no one but Jews. But there were some men from Cyprus and Cyrene among them who came to Antioch and began to speak to the Greeks too, proclaiming the good news of the Lord Jesus. The hand of the Lord was with them, and a great number who believed turned to the Lord. A report about them came to the attention of the church in Jerusalem, and they sent Barnabas to Antioch. When he came and saw the grace of God, he rejoiced and encouraged them all to remain true to the Lord with devoted hearts, because he was a good man, full of the Holy Spirit and of faith, and a significant number of people were brought to the Lord. Then Barnabas departed for Tarsus to look for Saul, and when he found him, he brought him to Antioch. So for a whole year Barnabas and Saul met with the church and taught a significant number of people. Now it was in Antioch that the disciples were first called Christians.

FAMINE RELIEF FOR JUDEA

At that time some prophets came down from Jerusalem to Antioch. One of them, named Agabus, got up and predicted by the Spirit that a severe famine was about to come over the whole inhabited world. (This took place during the reign of Claudius.) So the disciples, each in accordance with his financial ability, decided to send relief to the brothers living in Judea. They did so, sending their financial aid to the elders by Barnabas and Saul.

CHAPTER 12

JAMES IS KILLED AND PETER IMPRISONED

About that time King Herod laid hands on some from the church to harm them. He had James, the brother of John, executed with a sword. When he saw that this pleased the Jews, he proceeded to arrest Peter too. (This took place during the feast of Unleavened Bread.) When he had seized him, he put him in prison, handing him over to four squads of soldiers to guard him. Herod planned to bring him out for public trial after the Passover. So Peter was kept in prison, but those in the church were earnestly praying to God for him. On that very night before Herod was going to bring him out for trial, Peter was sleeping between two soldiers, bound with two chains, while guards in front of the door were keeping watch over the prison. Suddenly an angel of the Lord appeared, and a light shone in the prison cell. He struck Peter on the side and woke him up, saying, "Get up quickly!" And the chains fell off Peter's wrists. The angel said to him, "Fasten your belt and put on your sandals." Peter did so. Then the angel said to him, "Put on your cloak and follow me." Peter went out and followed him; he did not realize that what was happening through the angel was real, but thought he was seeing a vision. After they had passed the first and second guards, they came to the iron gate leading into the city. It opened for them by itself, and they went outside and walked down one narrow street, when at once the angel left him. When Peter came to himself, he said, "Now I know for certain that the Lord has sent his angel and rescued me from the hand of Herod and from everything the Jewish people were expecting to happen."

When Peter realized this, he went to the house of Mary, the mother of John Mark, where many people had gathered together and were praying. When he knocked at the door of the outer gate, a slave girl named Rhoda answered. When she recognized Peter's voice, she was so overjoyed she did not open the gate, but ran back in and told them that Peter was standing at the gate. But they said to her, "You've lost your mind!" But she kept insisting that it was Peter, and they kept saying, "It is his angel!" Now Peter continued knocking, and when they opened the door and saw him, they were greatly astonished. He motioned to them with his hand to be quiet and then related how the Lord had brought him out of the prison. He said, "Tell James and the brothers these things," and then he left and went to another place.

At daybreak there was great consternation among the soldiers over what had become of Peter. When Herod had searched for him and did not find him, he questioned the guards and commanded that they be led away to execution. Then Herod went down from Judea to Caesarea and stayed there.

Now Herod was having an angry quarrel with the people of Tyre and Sidon. So they joined together and presented themselves before him. And after convincing Blastus, the king's personal assistant, to help them, they asked for peace because their country's food supply was provided by the king's country. On a day determined in advance, Herod put on his royal robes, sat down on the judgment seat, and made a speech to them. But the crowd began to shout, "The voice of a god, and not of a man!" Immediately an angel of the Lord struck Herod down because he did not give the glory to God, and he was eaten by worms and died. But the word of God kept on increasing and multiplying.

So Barnabas and Saul returned to Jerusalem when they had completed their mission, bringing along with them John Mark.

CHAPTER 13

THE CHURCH AT ANTIOCH COMMISSIONS BARNABAS AND SAUL

Now there were these prophets and teachers in the church at Antioch: Barnabas, Simeon called Niger, Lucius the Cyrenian, Manaen (a close friend of Herod the tetrarch from childhood) and Saul. While they were serving the Lord and fasting, the Holy Spirit said, "Set apart for me Barnabas and Saul for the work to which I have called them." Then, after they had fasted and prayed and placed their hands on them, they sent them off.

PAUL AND BARNABAS PREACH IN CYPRUS

So Barnabas and Saul, sent out by the Holy Spirit, went down to Seleucia, and from there they sailed to Cyprus. When they arrived in Salamis, they began to proclaim the word of God in the Jewish synagogues. (Now they also had John as their assistant.) When they had crossed over the whole island as far as Paphos, they found a magician, a Jewish false prophet named Bar-Jesus, who was with the proconsul Sergius Paulus, an intelligent man. The proconsul summoned Barnabas and Saul and wanted to hear the word of God. But the magician Elymas (for that is the way his name is translated) opposed them, trying to turn the proconsul away from the faith. But Saul (also known as Paul), filled with the Holy Spirit, stared straight at him and said, "You who are full of all deceit and all wrongdoing, you son of the devil, you enemy of all righteousness—will you not stop making crooked the straight paths of the Lord? Now look, the hand of the Lord is against you, and you will be blind, unable to see the sun for a time!" Immediately mistiness and darkness came over him, and he went around seeking people to lead him by the hand. Then when the proconsul saw what had happened, he believed because he was greatly astounded at the teaching about the Lord.

PAUL AND BARNABAS AT PISIDIAN ANTIOCH

Then Paul and his companions put out to sea from Paphos and came to Perga in Pamphylia, but John left them and returned to Jerusalem. Moving on from Perga, they arrived at Pisidian Antioch, and on the Sabbath day they went into the synagogue and sat down. After the reading from the law and the prophets, the leaders of the synagogue sent them a message, saying, "Brothers, if you have any message of exhortation for the people, speak it." So Paul stood up, gestured with his hand and said,

"Men of Israel, and you Gentiles who fear God, listen: The God of this people Israel chose our ancestors and made the people great during their stay as foreigners in the country of Egypt, and with uplifted arm he led them out of it. For a period of about forty years he put up with them in the wilderness. After he had destroyed seven nations in the land of Canaan, he gave his people their land as an inheritance. All this took about 450 years. After this he gave them judges until the time of Samuel the prophet. Then they asked for a king, and God gave them Saul son of Kish, a man from the tribe of Benjamin, who ruled forty years. After removing him, God raised up David their king. He testified about him: '*I have found David* the son of Jesse *to be a man after my heart,* who will accomplish everything I want him to do.' From the descendants of this man God brought to Israel a Savior, Jesus, just as he promised. Before Jesus arrived, John had proclaimed a baptism for repentance to all the people of Israel. But while John was completing his mission, he said repeatedly, 'What do you think I am? I am not he. But look, one is coming after me. I am not worthy to untie the sandals on his feet!' Brothers, descendants of Abraham's family, and those Gentiles among you who fear God, the message of this salvation has been sent to us. For the people who live in Jerusalem and their rulers did not recognize him, and they fulfilled the sayings of the prophets that are read every Sabbath by condemning him. Though they found no basis for a death sentence, they asked Pilate to have him executed. When they had accomplished everything that was written about him, they took him down from the cross and placed him in a tomb. But God raised him from the dead, and for many days he appeared to those who had accompanied him from Galilee to Jerusalem. These are now his witnesses to the people. And we proclaim to you the good news about the promise to our ancestors, that this promise God has fulfilled to us, their children, by raising Jesus, as also it is written in the second psalm, *'You are my Son; today I have fathered you.'* But regarding the fact that he has raised Jesus from the dead, never again to be in a state of decay, God has spoken in this way: *'I will give you the holy and trustworthy promises made to David.'* Therefore he also says in another psalm, *'You will not permit your Holy One to experience decay.'* For David, after he had served God's purpose in his own generation, died, was buried with his ancestors, and experienced decay, but the one whom God raised up did not experience decay. Therefore let it be known to you, brothers, that through this one forgiveness of sins is proclaimed to you, and by this one everyone who believes is justified from everything from which the law of Moses could not justify you. Watch out, then, that what is spoken about by the prophets does not happen to you:

'Look, you scoffers; be amazed and perish! For I am doing a work in your days,

*a work you would never believe, even if
someone tells you.'* "

As Paul and Barnabas were going out, the people were urging them to speak about these things on the next Sabbath. When the meeting of the synagogue had broken up, many of the Jews and God-fearing proselytes followed Paul and Barnabas, who were speaking with them and were persuading them to continue in the grace of God.

On the next Sabbath almost the whole city assembled together to hear the word of the Lord. But when the Jews saw the crowds, they were filled with jealousy, and they began to contradict what Paul was saying by reviling him. Both Paul and Barnabas replied courageously, "It was necessary to speak the word of God to you first. Since you reject it and do not consider yourselves worthy of eternal life, we are turning to the Gentiles. For this is what the Lord has commanded us: *'I have appointed you to be a light for the Gentiles, to bring salvation to the ends of the earth.'* " When the Gentiles heard this, they began to rejoice and praise the word of the Lord, and all who had been appointed for eternal life believed. So the word of the Lord was spreading through the entire region. But the Jews incited the God-fearing women of high social standing and the prominent men of the city, stirred up persecution against Paul and Barnabas, and threw them out of their region. So after they shook the dust off their feet in protest against them, they went to Iconium. And the disciples were filled with joy and with the Holy Spirit.

CHAPTER 14

PAUL AND BARNABAS AT ICONIUM

The same thing happened in Iconium when Paul and Barnabas went into the Jewish synagogue and spoke in such a way that a large group of both Jews and Greeks believed. But the Jews who refused to believe stirred up the Gentiles and poisoned their minds against the brothers. So they stayed there for a considerable time, speaking out courageously for the Lord, who testified to the message of his grace, granting miraculous signs and wonders to be performed through their hands. But the population of the city was divided; some sided with the Jews, and some with the apostles. When both the Gentiles and the Jews (together with their rulers) made an attempt to mistreat them and stone them, Paul and Barnabas learned about it and fled to the Lycaonian cities of Lystra and Derbe and the surrounding region. There they continued to proclaim the good news.

PAUL AND BARNABAS AT LYSTRA

In Lystra sat a man who could not use his feet, lame from birth, who had never walked. This man was listening to Paul as he was speaking. When Paul stared intently at him and saw he had faith to be healed, he said with a loud voice, "Stand upright on your feet." And the man leaped up and began walking. So when the crowds saw what Paul had done, they shouted in the Lycaonian language, "The gods have come down to us in human form!" They began to call Barnabas Zeus and Paul Hermes, because he was the chief speaker. The priest of the temple of Zeus, located just outside the city, brought bulls and garlands to the city gates; he and the crowds wanted to offer sacrifices to them. But when the apostles Barnabas and Paul heard about it, they tore their clothes and rushed out into the crowd, shouting, "Men, why are you doing these things? We too are men, with human natures just like you! We are proclaiming the good news to you, so that you should turn from these worthless things to the living God, who made the heaven, the earth, the sea, and everything that is in them. In past generations he allowed all the nations to go their own ways, yet he did not leave himself without a witness by doing good, by giving you rain from heaven and fruitful seasons, satisfying you with food and your hearts with joy." Even by saying these things, they scarcely persuaded the crowds not to offer sacrifice to them.

But Jews came from Antioch and Iconium, and after winning the crowds over, they stoned Paul and dragged him out of the city, presuming him to be dead. But after the disciples had surrounded him, he got up and went back into the city. On the next day he left with Barnabas for Derbe.

PAUL AND BARNABAS RETURN TO ANTIOCH IN SYRIA

After they had proclaimed the good news in that city and made many disciples, they returned to Lystra, to Iconium, and to Antioch. They strengthened the souls of the disciples and encouraged them to continue in the faith, saying, "We must enter the kingdom of God through many persecutions." When they had appointed elders for them in the various churches, with prayer and fasting they entrusted them to the protection of the Lord in whom they had believed. Then they passed through Pisidia and came into Pamphylia, and when they had spoken the word in Perga, they went down to Attalia. From there they sailed back to Antioch, where they had been commended to the grace of God for the work they had now completed. When they arrived and gathered the church together, they reported all the things God had done with them, and that he had opened a door of faith for the Gentiles. So they spent considerable time with the disciples.

CHAPTER 15

THE JERUSALEM COUNCIL

Now some men came down from Judea and began to teach the brothers, "Unless you are circumcised according to the custom of Moses, you cannot be saved." When Paul and Barnabas had a major argument and debate with them, the church appointed Paul and Barnabas and some others from among them to go up to meet with the apostles and elders in Jerusalem about this point of disagreement. So they were sent on their way by the church, and as they passed through both Phoenicia and Samaria, they were relating at length the conversion of the Gentiles and bringing great joy to all the brothers. When they arrived in Jerusalem, they were received by the church and the apostles and the elders, and they reported all the things God had done with them. But some from the religious party of the Pharisees who had believed stood up and said, "It is necessary to circumcise the Gentiles and to order them to observe the law of Moses."

Both the apostles and the elders met together to deliberate about this matter. After there had been much debate, Peter stood up and said to them, "Brothers, you know that some time ago God chose me to preach to the Gentiles so they would hear the message of the gospel and believe. And God, who knows the heart, has testified to them by giving them the Holy Spirit just as he did to us, and he made no distinction between them and us, cleansing their hearts by faith. So now why are you putting God to the test by placing on the neck of the disciples a yoke that neither our ancestors nor we have been able to bear? On the contrary, we believe that we are saved through the grace of the Lord Jesus, in the same way as they are."

The whole group kept quiet and listened to Barnabas and Paul while they explained all the miraculous signs and wonders God had done among the Gentiles through them. After they stopped speaking, James replied, "Brothers, listen to me. Simeon has explained how God first concerned himself to select from among the Gentiles a people for his name. The words of the prophets agree with this, as it is written,

'After this I will return,
and I will rebuild the fallen tent of David;
I will rebuild its ruins and restore it,
so that the rest of humanity may seek
    the Lord,
namely, all the Gentiles I have called to be
    my own,' says the Lord, who makes these
things known from long ago.

"Therefore I conclude that we should not cause extra difficulty for those among the Gentiles who are turning to God, but that we should write them a letter telling them to abstain from things defiled by idols and from sexual immorality and from what has been strangled and from blood. For Moses has had those who proclaim him in every town from ancient times, because he is read aloud in the synagogues every Sabbath."

Then the apostles and elders, with the whole church, decided to send men chosen from among them, Judas called Barsabbas and Silas, leaders among the brothers, to Antioch with Paul and Barnabas. They sent this letter with them:

From the apostles and elders, your brothers, to the Gentile brothers and sisters in Antioch, Syria, and Cilicia, greetings! Since we have heard that some have gone out from among us with no orders from us and have confused you, upsetting your minds by what they said, we have unanimously decided to choose men to send to you along with our dear friends Barnabas and Paul, who have risked their lives for the name of our Lord Jesus Christ. Therefore we are sending Judas and Silas who will tell you these things themselves in person. For it seemed best to the Holy Spirit and to us not to place any greater burden on you than these necessary rules: that you abstain from meat that has been sacrificed to idols and from blood and from what has been strangled and from sexual immorality. If you keep yourselves from doing these things, you will do well. Farewell.

So when they were dismissed, they went down to Antioch, and after gathering the entire group together, they delivered the letter. When they read it aloud, the people rejoiced at its encouragement. Both Judas and Silas, who were prophets themselves, encouraged and strengthened the brothers with a long speech. After they had spent some time there, they were sent off in peace by the brothers to those who had sent them. But Paul and Barnabas remained in Antioch, teaching and proclaiming (along with many others) the word of the Lord.

PAUL AND BARNABAS PART COMPANY

After some days Paul said to Barnabas, "Let's return and visit the brothers in every town where we proclaimed the word of the Lord to see how they are doing." Barnabas wanted to bring John called Mark along with them too, but Paul insisted that they should not take along this one who had left them in Pamphylia and had not accompanied them in the work. They had a sharp disagreement, so that they parted company. Barnabas took along Mark and sailed away to Cyprus, but Paul chose Silas and set out, commended to the grace of the Lord by the brothers and sisters. He passed through Syria and Cilicia, strengthening the churches.

CHAPTER 16

TIMOTHY JOINS PAUL AND SILAS

He also came to Derbe and to Lystra. A disciple named Timothy was there, the son of a Jewish woman who was a believer, but whose father was a Greek. The brothers in Lystra and Iconium spoke well of him. Paul wanted Timothy to accompany him, and he took him and circumcised him because of the Jews who were in those places, for they all knew that his father was Greek. As they went through the towns, they passed on the decrees that had been decided on by the apostles and elders in Jerusalem for the Gentile believers to obey. So the churches were being strengthened in the faith and were increasing in number every day.

PAUL'S VISION OF THE MACEDONIAN MAN

They went through the region of Phrygia and Galatia, having been prevented by the Holy Spirit from speaking the message in the province of Asia. When they came to Mysia, they attempted to go into Bithynia, but the Spirit of Jesus did not allow them to do this, so they passed through Mysia and went down to Troas. A vision appeared to Paul during the night: A Macedonian man was standing there urging him, "Come over to Macedonia and help us!" After Paul saw the vision, we attempted immediately to go over to Macedonia, concluding that God had called us to proclaim the good news to them.

ARRIVAL AT PHILIPPI

We put out to sea from Troas and sailed a straight course to Samothrace, the next day to Neapolis, and from there to Philippi, which is a leading city of that district of Macedonia, a Roman colony. We stayed in this city for some days. On the Sabbath day we went outside the city gate to the side of the river, where we thought there would be a place of prayer, and we sat down and began to speak to the women who had assembled there. A woman named Lydia, a dealer in purple cloth from the city of Thyatira, a God-fearing woman, listened to us. The Lord opened her heart to respond to what Paul was saying. After she and her household were baptized, she urged us, "If you consider me to be a believer in the Lord, come and stay in my house." And she persuaded us.

PAUL AND SILAS ARE THROWN INTO PRISON

Now as we were going to the place of prayer, a slave girl met us who had a spirit that enabled her to foretell the future by supernatural means. She brought her owners a great profit by fortune-telling. She followed behind Paul and us and kept crying out, "These men are servants of the Most High God, who are proclaiming to you the way of salvation." She continued to do this for many days. But Paul became greatly annoyed, and turned and said to the spirit, "I command you in the name of Jesus Christ to come out of her!" And it came out of her at once. But when her owners saw their hope of profit was gone, they seized Paul and Silas and dragged them into the market-place before the authorities. When they had brought them before the magistrates, they said, "These men are throwing our city into confusion. They are Jews and are advocating customs that are not lawful for us to accept or practice, since we are Romans."

The crowd joined the attack against them, and the magistrates tore the clothes off Paul and Silas and ordered them to be beaten with rods. After they had beaten them severely, they threw them into prison and commanded the jailer to guard them securely. Receiving such orders, he threw them in the inner cell and fastened their feet in the stocks.

About midnight Paul and Silas were praying and singing hymns to God, and the rest of the prisoners were listening to them. Suddenly a great earthquake occurred, so that the foundations of the prison were shaken. Immediately all the doors flew open, and the bonds of all the prisoners came loose. When the jailer woke up and saw the doors of the prison standing open, he drew his sword and was about to kill himself because he assumed the prisoners had escaped. But Paul called out loudly, "Do not harm yourself, for we are all here!" Calling for lights, the jailer rushed in and fell down trembling at the feet of Paul and Silas. Then he brought them outside and asked, "Sirs, what must I do to be saved?" They replied, "Believe in the Lord Jesus and you will be saved, you and your household." Then they spoke the word of the Lord to him, along with all those who were in his house. At that hour of the night he took them and washed their wounds; then he and all his family were baptized right away. The jailer brought them into his house and set food before them, and he rejoiced greatly that he had come to believe in God, together with his entire household. At daybreak the magistrates sent their police officers, saying, "Release those men." The jailer reported these words to Paul, saying, "The magistrates have sent orders to release you. So come out now and go in peace." But Paul said to the police officers, "They had us beaten in public without a proper trial—even though we are Roman citizens—and they threw us in prison. And now they want to send us away secretly? Absolutely not! They themselves must come and escort us out!" The police officers reported these words to the magistrates. They were frightened when they heard Paul and Silas were Roman citizens and came and apologized to them. After they brought them out, they asked them repeatedly to leave the city. When they came out of the prison, they entered Lydia's house, and when they saw the brothers, they encouraged them and then departed.

CHAPTER 17

PAUL AND SILAS AT THESSALONICA

After they traveled through Amphipolis and Apollonia, they came to Thessalonica, where there was a Jewish synagogue. Paul went to the Jews in the synagogue, as he customarily did, and on three Sabbath days he addressed them from the scriptures, explaining and demonstrating that the Christ had to suffer and to rise from the dead, saying, "This Jesus I am proclaiming to you is the Christ." Some of them were persuaded and joined Paul and Silas, along with a large group of God-fearing Greeks and quite a few prominent women. But the Jews became jealous, and gathering together some worthless men from the rabble in the marketplace, they formed a mob and set the city in an uproar. They attacked Jason's house, trying to find Paul and Silas to bring them out to the assembly. When they did not find them, they dragged Jason and some of the brothers before the city officials, screaming, "These people who have stirred up trouble throughout the world have come here too, and Jason has welcomed them as guests! They are all acting against Caesar's decrees, saying there is another king named Jesus!" They caused confusion among the crowd and the city officials who heard these things. After the city officials had received bail from Jason and the others, they released them.

PAUL AND SILAS AT BEREA

The brothers sent Paul and Silas off to Berea at once, during the night. When they arrived, they went to the Jewish synagogue. These Jews were more open-minded than those in Thessalonica, for they eagerly received the message, examining the scriptures carefully every day to see if these things were so. Therefore many of them believed, along with quite a few prominent Greek women and men. But when the Jews from Thessalonica heard that Paul had also proclaimed the word of God in Berea, they came there too, inciting and disturbing the crowds. Then the brothers sent Paul away to the coast at once, but Silas and Timothy remained in Berea. Those who accompanied Paul escorted him as far as Athens, and after receiving an order for Silas and Timothy to come to him as soon as possible, they left.

PAUL AT ATHENS

While Paul was waiting for them in Athens, his spirit was greatly upset because he saw the city was full of idols. So he was addressing the Jews and the God-fearing Gentiles in the synagogue, and in the marketplace every day those who happened to be there. Also some of the Epicurean and Stoic philosophers were conversing with him, and some were asking, "What does this foolish babbler want to say?" Others said, "He seems to be a proclaimer of foreign gods." (They said this because he was proclaiming the good news about Jesus and the resurrection.) So they took Paul and brought him to the Areopagus, saying, "May we know what this new teaching is that you are proclaiming? For you are bringing some surprising things to our ears, so we want to know what they mean." (All the Athenians and the foreigners who lived there used to spend their time in nothing else than telling or listening to something new.)

So Paul stood before the Areopagus and said, "Men of Athens, I see that you are very religious in all respects. For as I went around and observed closely your objects of worship, I even found an altar with this inscription: 'To an unknown god.' Therefore what you worship without knowing it, this I proclaim to you. The God who made the world and everything in it, who is Lord of heaven and earth, does not live in temples made by human hands, nor is he served by human hands, as if he needed anything, because he himself gives life and breath and everything to everyone. From one man he made every nation of the human race to inhabit the entire earth, determining their set times and the fixed limits of the places where they would live, so that they would search for God and perhaps grope around for him and find him, though he is not far from each one of us. For in him we live and move about and exist, as even some of your own poets have said, 'For we too are his offspring.' So since we are God's offspring, we should not think the deity is like gold or silver or stone, an image made by human skill and imagination. Therefore, although God has overlooked such times of ignorance, he now commands all people everywhere to repent, because he has set a day on which he is going to judge the world in righteousness, by a man whom he designated, having provided proof to everyone by raising him from the dead."

Now when they heard about the resurrection from the dead, some began to scoff, but others said, "We will hear you again about this." So Paul left the Areopagus. But some people joined him and believed. Among them were Dionysius, who was a member of the Areopagus, a woman named Damaris, and others with them.

CHAPTER 18

PAUL AT CORINTH

After this Paul departed from Athens and went to Corinth. There he found a Jew named Aquila, a native of Pontus, who had recently come from Italy with his wife Priscilla, because Claudius had ordered all the Jews to depart from Rome. Paul approached them, and because he worked at the same trade, he stayed with them and worked with them (for they were tentmakers by trade). He addressed both Jews and Greeks in the synagogue every Sabbath, attempting to persuade them.

Now when Silas and Timothy arrived from Macedonia, Paul became wholly absorbed with proclaiming the word, testifying to the Jews that Jesus was the Christ. When they opposed him and reviled him, he protested by shaking out his clothes and said to them, "Your blood be on your own heads! I am guiltless! From now on I will go to the Gentiles!" Then Paul left the synagogue and went to the house of a person named Titius Justus, a Gentile who worshiped God, whose house was next door to the synagogue. Crispus, the president of the synagogue, believed in the Lord together with his entire household, and many of the Corinthians who heard about it believed and were baptized. The Lord said to Paul by a vision in the night, "Do not be afraid, but speak and do not be silent because I am with you, and no one will assault you to harm you because I have many people in this city." So he stayed there a year and six months, teaching the word of God among them.

PAUL BEFORE THE PROCONSUL GALLIO

Now while Gallio was proconsul of Achaia, the Jews attacked Paul together and brought him before the judgment seat, saying, "This man is persuading people to worship God in a way contrary to the law!" But just as Paul was about to speak, Gallio said to the Jews, "If it were a matter of some crime or serious piece of villainy, I would have been justified in accepting the complaint of you Jews, but since it concerns points of disagreement about words and names and your own law, settle it yourselves. I will not be a judge of these things!" Then he had them forced away from the judgment seat. So they all seized Sosthenes, the president of the synagogue, and began to beat him in front of the judgment seat. Yet none of these things were of any concern to Gallio.

PAUL RETURNS TO ANTIOCH IN SYRIA

Paul, after staying many more days in Corinth, said farewell to the brothers and sailed away to Syria accompanied by Priscilla and Aquila. He had his hair cut off at Cenchrea because he had made a vow. When they reached Ephesus, Paul left Priscilla and Aquila behind there, but he himself went into the synagogue and addressed the Jews. When they asked him to stay longer, he would not consent, but said farewell to them and added, "I will come back to you again if God wills." Then he set sail from Ephesus, and when he arrived at Caesarea, he went up and greeted the church at Jerusalem and then went down to Antioch. After he spent some time there, Paul left and went through the region of Galatia and Phrygia, strengthening all the disciples.

APOLLOS BEGINS HIS MINISTRY

Now a Jew named Apollos, a native of Alexandria, arrived in Ephesus. He was an eloquent speaker, well-versed in the scriptures. He had been instructed in the way of the Lord, and with great enthusiasm he spoke and taught accurately the facts about Jesus, although he knew only the baptism of John. He began to speak out fearlessly in the synagogue, but when Priscilla and Aquila heard him, they took him aside and explained the way of God to him more accurately. When Apollos wanted to cross over to Achaia, the brothers encouraged him and wrote to the disciples to welcome him. When he arrived, he assisted greatly those who had believed by grace, for he refuted the Jews vigorously in public debate, demonstrating from the scriptures that the Christ was Jesus.

CHAPTER 19

DISCIPLES OF JOHN THE BAPTIST AT EPHESUS

While Apollos was in Corinth, Paul went through the inland regions and came to Ephesus. He found some disciples there and said to them, "Did you receive the Holy Spirit when you believed?" They replied, "No, we have not even heard that there is a Holy Spirit." So Paul said, "Into what then were you baptized?" "Into John's baptism," they replied. Paul said, "John baptized with a baptism of repentance, telling the people to believe in the one who was to come after him, that is, in Jesus." When they heard this, they were baptized in the name of the Lord Jesus, and when Paul placed his hands on them, the Holy Spirit came upon them, and they began to speak in tongues and to prophesy. (Now there were about 12 men in all.)

PAUL CONTINUES TO MINISTER AT EPHESUS

So Paul entered the synagogue and spoke out fearlessly for three months, addressing and convincing them about the kingdom of God. But when some were stubborn and refused to believe, reviling the Way before the congregation, he left them and took the disciples with him, addressing them every day in the lecture hall of Tyrannus. This went on for two years, so that all who lived in the province of Asia, both Jews and Greeks, heard the word of the Lord.

THE SEVEN SONS OF SCEVA

God was performing extraordinary miracles by Paul's hands, so that when even handkerchiefs or aprons that had touched his body were brought to the sick, their diseases left them and the evil spirits went out of them. But some itinerant Jewish exorcists tried to invoke the name of the Lord Jesus over those who were possessed by evil spirits, saying, "I sternly warn you by Jesus whom Paul preaches." (Now seven sons of a man named Sceva, a Jewish high priest, were doing this.) But the evil spirit replied to them, "I know about Jesus and I am acquainted with Paul, but who are you?" Then the man who was possessed by the evil spirit jumped on them and beat them all into submission. He prevailed against them so that they fled from that house naked and wounded. This became known to all who lived in Ephesus, both Jews and Greeks; fear came over them all, and the name of the Lord Jesus was praised. Many of those who had believed came forward, confessing and making their deeds known. Large numbers of those who had practiced magic collected their books and burned them up in the presence of everyone. When the value of the books was added up, it was found to total 50,000 silver coins. In this way the word of the Lord continued to grow in power and to prevail.

A RIOT IN EPHESUS

Now after all these things had taken place, Paul resolved to go to Jerusalem, passing through Macedonia and Achaia. He said, "After I have been there, I must also see Rome." So after sending two of his assistants, Timothy and Erastus, to Macedonia, he himself stayed on for a while in the province of Asia.

At that time a great disturbance took place concerning the Way. For a man named Demetrius, a silversmith who made silver shrines of Artemis, brought a great deal of business to the craftsmen. He gathered these together, along with the workmen in similar trades, and said, "Men, you know that our prosperity comes from this business. And you see and hear that this Paul has persuaded and turned away a large crowd, not only in Ephesus but in practically all of the province of Asia, by saying that gods made by hands are not gods at all. There is danger not only that this business of ours will come into disrepute, but also that the temple of the great goddess Artemis will be regarded as nothing, and she whom all the province of Asia and the world worship will suffer the loss of her greatness."

When they heard this they became enraged and began to shout, "Great is Artemis of the Ephesians!" The city was filled with the uproar, and the crowd rushed to the theater together, dragging with them Gaius and Aristarchus, the Macedonians who were Paul's traveling companions. But when Paul wanted to enter the public assembly, the disciples would not let him. Even some of the provincial authorities who were his friends sent a message to him, urging him not to venture into the theater. So then some were shouting one thing, some another, for the assembly was in confusion, and most of them did not know why they had met together. Some of the crowd concluded it was about Alexander because the Jews had pushed him to the front. Alexander, gesturing with his hand, was wanting to make a defense before the public assembly. But when they recognized that he was a Jew, they all shouted in unison, "Great is Artemis of the Ephesians!" for about two hours. After the city secretary quieted the crowd, he said, "Men of Ephesus, what person is there who does not know that the city of the Ephesians is the keeper of the temple of the great Artemis and of her image that fell from heaven? So because these facts are indisputable, you must keep quiet and not do anything reckless. For you have brought these men here who are neither temple robbers nor blasphemers of our goddess. If then Demetrius and the craftsmen who are with him have a complaint against someone, the courts are open and there are proconsuls; let them bring charges against one another there. But if you want anything in addition, it will have to be settled in a legal assembly. For we are in danger of being charged with rioting today, since there is no cause we can give to explain this disorderly gathering." After he had said this, he dismissed the assembly.

CHAPTER 20

PAUL TRAVELS THROUGH MACEDONIA AND GREECE

After the disturbance had ended, Paul sent for the disciples, and after encouraging them and saying farewell, he left to go to

Macedonia. After he had gone through those regions and spoken many words of encouragement to the believers there, he came to Greece, where he stayed for three months. Because the Jews had made a plot against him as he was intending to sail for Syria, he decided to return through Macedonia. Paul was accompanied by Sopater son of Pyrrhus from Berea, Aristarchus and Secundus from Thessalonica, Gaius from Derbe, and Timothy, as well as Tychicus and Trophimus from the province of Asia. These had gone on ahead and were waiting for us in Troas. We sailed away from Philippi after the days of Unleavened Bread, and within five days we came to the others in Troas, where we stayed for seven days. On the first day of the week, when we met to break bread, Paul began to speak to the people, and because he intended to leave the next day, he extended his message until midnight. (Now there were many lamps in the upstairs room where we were meeting.) A young man named Eutychus, who was sitting in the window, was sinking into a deep sleep while Paul continued to speak for a long time. Fast asleep, he fell down from the third story and was picked up dead. But Paul went down, threw himself on the young man, put his arms around him, and said, "Do not be distressed, for he is still alive!" Then Paul went back upstairs, and after he had broken bread and eaten, he talked with them a long time, until dawn. Then he left. They took the boy home alive and were greatly comforted.

THE VOYAGE TO MILETUS

We went on ahead to the ship and put out to sea for Assos, intending to take Paul aboard there, for he had arranged it this way. He himself was intending to go there by land. When he met us in Assos, we took him aboard and went to Mitylene. We set sail from there, and on the following day we arrived off Chios. The next day we approached Samos, and the day after that we arrived at Miletus. For Paul had decided to sail past Ephesus so as not to spend time in the province of Asia, for he was hurrying to arrive in Jerusalem, if possible, by the day of Pentecost. From Miletus he sent a message to Ephesus, telling the elders of the church to come to him.

When they arrived, he said to them, "You yourselves know how I lived the whole time I was with you, from the first day I set foot in the province of Asia, serving the Lord with all humility and with tears, and with the trials that happened to me because of the plots of the Jews. You know that I did not hold back from proclaiming to you anything that would be helpful, and from teaching you publicly and from house to house, testifying to both Jews and Greeks about repentance toward God and faith in our Lord Jesus. And now, compelled by the Spirit, I am going to Jerusalem without knowing what will happen to me there, except that the Holy Spirit warns me in town after town that imprisonment and persecutions are waiting for me. But I do not consider my life worth anything to myself, so that I may finish my task and the ministry that I received from the Lord Jesus, to testify to the good news of God's grace.

"And now I know that none of you among whom I went around proclaiming the kingdom will see me again. Therefore I declare to you today that I am innocent of the blood of you all. For I did not hold back from announcing to you the whole purpose of God. Watch out for yourselves and for all the flock of which the Holy Spirit has made you overseers, to shepherd the church of God that he obtained with the blood of his own Son. I know that after I am gone fierce wolves will come in among you, not sparing the flock. Even from among your own group men will arise, teaching perversions of the truth to draw the disciples away after them. Therefore be alert, remembering that night and day for three years I did not stop warning each one of you with tears. And now I entrust you to God and to the message of his grace. This message is able to build you up and give you an inheritance among all those who are sanctified. I have desired no one's silver or gold or clothing. You yourselves know that these hands of mine provided for my needs and the needs of those who were with me. By all these things, I have shown you that by working in this way we must help the weak, and remember the words of the Lord Jesus that he himself said, 'It is more blessed to give than to receive.'"

When he had said these things, he knelt down with them all and prayed. They all began to weep loudly, and hugged Paul and kissed him, especially saddened by what he had said, that they were not going to see him again. Then they accompanied him to the ship.

CHAPTER 21

PAUL'S JOURNEY TO JERUSALEM

After we tore ourselves away from them, we put out to sea, and sailing a straight course, we came to Cos, on the next day to Rhodes, and from there to Patara. We found a ship crossing over to Phoenicia, went aboard, and put out to sea. After we sighted Cyprus and left it behind on our port side, we sailed on to Syria and put in at Tyre because the ship was to unload its cargo there. After we located the disciples, we stayed there seven days. They repeatedly told Paul through the Spirit not to set foot in Jerusalem. When our time was over, we left and went on our way. All of them, with their wives and children, accompanied us outside of the city. After kneeling down on the beach and praying, we said farewell to one another. Then we went aboard the ship, and they returned to their own homes. We continued the voyage from Tyre and arrived at Ptolemais, and when we had greeted the brothers, we stayed with them for one day. On the next day we left and came to Caesarea, and entered the house of Philip the evangelist, who was one of the seven, and stayed with him. (He had four unmarried daughters who prophesied.)

While we remained there for a number of days, a prophet named Agabus came down from Judea. He came to us, took Paul's belt, tied his own hands and feet with it, and said, "The Holy Spirit says this: 'This is the way the Jews in Jerusalem will tie up the man whose belt this is and will hand him over to the Gentiles.'" When we heard this, both we and the local people begged him not to go up to Jerusalem. Then Paul replied, "What are you doing, weeping and breaking my heart? For I am ready not only to be tied up, but even to die in Jerusalem for the name of the Lord Jesus." Because he could not be persuaded, we said no more except, "The Lord's will be done."

After these days we got ready and started up to Jerusalem. Some of the disciples from Caesarea came along with us too, and brought us to the house of Mnason of Cyprus, a disciple from the earliest times, with whom we were to stay. When we arrived in Jerusalem, the brothers welcomed us gladly. The next day Paul went in with us to see James, and all the elders were there. When Paul had greeted them, he began to explain in detail what God had done among the Gentiles through his ministry. When they heard this, they praised God. Then they said to him, "You see, brother, how many thousands of Jews there are who have believed, and they are all ardent observers of the law. They have been informed about you—that you teach all the Jews now living among the Gentiles to abandon Moses, telling them not to circumcise their children or live according to our customs. What then should we do? They will no doubt hear that you have come. So do what we tell you: We have four men who have taken a vow; take them and purify yourself along with them and pay their expenses, so that they may have their heads shaved. Then everyone will know there is nothing in what they have been told about you, but that you yourself live in conformity with the law. But regarding the Gentiles who have believed, we have written a letter, having decided that they should avoid meat that has been sacrificed to idols and blood and what has been strangled and sexual immorality." Then Paul took the men the next day, and after he had purified himself along with them, he went to the temple and gave notice of the completion of the days of purification, when the sacrifice would be offered for each of them. When the seven days

were almost over, the Jews from the province
of Asia who had seen him in the temple area
stirred up the whole crowd and seized him,
shouting, "Men of Israel, help! This is the man
who teaches everyone everywhere against
our people, our law, and this sanctuary! Furthermore he has brought Greeks into the inner courts of the temple and made this holy
place ritually unclean!" (For they had seen
Trophimus the Ephesian in the city with
him previously, and they assumed Paul had
brought him into the inner temple courts.)
The whole city was stirred up, and the people rushed together. They seized Paul and
dragged him out of the temple courts, and
immediately the doors were shut. While they
were trying to kill him, a report was sent up to
the commanding officer of the cohort that all
Jerusalem was in confusion. He immediately
took soldiers and centurions and ran down to
the crowd. When they saw the commanding
officer and the soldiers, they stopped beating
Paul. Then the commanding officer came up
and arrested him and ordered him to be tied
up with two chains; he then asked who he was
and what he had done. But some in the crowd
shouted one thing, and others something
else, and when the commanding officer was
unable to find out the truth because of the
disturbance, he ordered Paul to be brought
into the barracks. When he came to the steps,
Paul had to be carried by the soldiers because

of the violence of the mob, for a crowd of people followed them, screaming, "Away with him!" As Paul was about to be brought into the barracks, he said to the commanding officer, "May I say something to you?" The officer replied, "Do you know Greek? Then you're not that Egyptian who started a rebellion and led the 4,000 men of the 'Assassins' into the wilderness sometime ago?" Paul answered, "I am a Jew from Tarsus in Cilicia, a citizen of an important city. Please allow me to speak to the people." When the commanding officer had given him permission, Paul stood on the steps and gestured to the people with his hand. When they had become silent, he addressed them in Aramaic,

CHAPTER 22

PAUL'S DEFENSE

"Brothers and fathers, listen to my defense that I now make to you." (When they heard that he was addressing them in Aramaic, they became even quieter.) Then Paul said, "I am a Jew, born in Tarsus in Cilicia, but brought up in this city, educated with strictness under Gamaliel according to the law of our ancestors, and was zealous for God just as all of you are today. I persecuted this Way even to the point of death, tying up both men and women and putting them in prison, as both the high priest and the whole council of elders can testify about me. From them I also received letters to the brothers in Damascus, and I was on my way to make arrests there and bring the prisoners to Jerusalem to be punished. As I was en route and near Damascus, about noon a very bright light from heaven suddenly flashed around me. Then I fell to the ground and heard a voice saying to me, 'Saul, Saul, why are you persecuting me?' I answered, 'Who are you, Lord?' He said to me, 'I am Jesus the Nazarene, whom you are persecuting.' Those who were with me saw the light, but did not understand the voice of the one who was speaking to me. So I asked, 'What should I do, Lord?' The Lord said to me, 'Get up and go to Damascus; there you will be told about everything that you have been designated to do.' Since I could not see because of the brilliance of that light, I came to Damascus led by the hand of those who were with me. A man named Ananias, a devout man according to the law, well spoken of by all the Jews who live there, came to me and stood beside me and said to me, 'Brother Saul, regain your sight!' And at that very moment I looked up and saw him. Then he said, 'The God of our ancestors has already chosen you to know his will, to see the Righteous One, and to hear a command from his mouth, because you will be his witness to all people of what you have seen and heard. And now what are you waiting for? Get up, be baptized, and have your sins washed away, calling on his name.' When

I returned to Jerusalem and was praying in the temple, I fell into a trance and saw the Lord saying to me, 'Hurry and get out of Jerusalem quickly because they will not accept your testimony about me.' I replied, 'Lord, they themselves know that I imprisoned and beat those in the various synagogues who believed in you. And when the blood of your witness Stephen was shed, I myself was standing nearby, approving, and guarding the cloaks of those who were killing him.' Then he said to me, 'Go, because I will send you far away to the Gentiles.'"

THE ROMAN COMMANDER QUESTIONS PAUL

The crowd was listening to him until he said this. Then they raised their voices and shouted, "Away with this man from the earth! For he should not be allowed to live!" While they were screaming and throwing off their cloaks and tossing dust in the air, the commanding officer ordered Paul to be brought back into the barracks. He told them to interrogate Paul by beating him with a lash so that he could find out the reason the crowd was shouting at Paul in this way. When they had stretched him out for the lash, Paul said to the centurion standing nearby, "Is it legal for you to lash a man who is a Roman citizen without a proper trial?" When the centurion heard this, he went to the commanding officer and reported it, saying, "What are you

about to do? For this man is a Roman citizen."
So the commanding officer came and asked
Paul, "Tell me, are you a Roman citizen?" He
replied, "Yes." The commanding officer answered, "I acquired this citizenship with a
large sum of money." "But I was even born a
citizen," Paul replied. Then those who were
about to interrogate him stayed away from
him, and the commanding officer was frightened when he realized that Paul was a Roman
citizen and that he had had him tied up.

PAUL BEFORE THE SANHEDRIN

The next day, because the commanding officer wanted to know the true reason Paul was
being accused by the Jews, he released him
and ordered the chief priests and the whole
council to assemble. He then brought Paul
down and had him stand before them.

CHAPTER 23

Paul looked directly at the council and said,
"Brothers, I have lived my life with a clear conscience before God to this day." At that the
high priest Ananias ordered those standing
near Paul to strike him on the mouth. Then
Paul said to him, "God is going to strike you,
you whitewashed wall! Do you sit there judging me according to the law, and in violation
of the law you order me to be struck?" Those
standing near him said, "Do you dare insult
God's high priest?" Paul replied, "I did not realize, brothers, that he was the high priest,

for it is written, '*You must not speak evil about a ruler of your people.*' "

Then when Paul noticed that part of them were Sadducees and the others Pharisees, he shouted out in the council, "Brothers, I am a Pharisee, a son of Pharisees. I am on trial concerning the hope of the resurrection of the dead!" When he said this, an argument began between the Pharisees and the Sadducees, and the assembly was divided. (For the Sadducees say there is no resurrection, or angel, or spirit, but the Pharisees acknowledge them all.) There was a great commotion, and some experts in the law from the party of the Pharisees stood up and protested strongly, "We find nothing wrong with this man. What if a spirit or an angel has spoken to him?" When the argument became so great the commanding officer feared that they would tear Paul to pieces, he ordered the detachment to go down, take him away from them by force, and bring him into the barracks.

The following night the Lord stood near Paul and said, "Have courage, for just as you have testified about me in Jerusalem, so you must also testify in Rome."

THE PLOT TO KILL PAUL

When morning came, the Jews formed a conspiracy and bound themselves with an oath not to eat or drink anything until they had killed Paul. There were more than forty of them who formed this conspiracy. They went to the chief priests and the elders and said, "We have bound ourselves with a solemn oath not to partake of anything until we have killed Paul. So now you and the council request the commanding officer to bring him down to you, as if you were going to determine his case by conducting a more thorough inquiry. We are ready to kill him before he comes near this place."

But when the son of Paul's sister heard about the ambush, he came and entered the barracks and told Paul. Paul called one of the centurions and said, "Take this young man to the commanding officer, for he has something to report to him." So the centurion took him and brought him to the commanding officer and said, "The prisoner Paul called me and asked me to bring this young man to you because he has something to tell you." The commanding officer took him by the hand, withdrew privately, and asked, "What is it that you want to report to me?" He replied, "The Jews have agreed to ask you to bring Paul down to the council tomorrow, as if they were going to inquire more thoroughly about him. So do not let them persuade you to do this because more than forty of them are lying in ambush for him. They have bound themselves with an oath not to eat or drink anything until they have killed him, and now they are ready, waiting for you to agree to their request." Then the commanding officer sent the young man away, directing him, "Tell no one that you have reported these things to me." Then he summoned two of the centurions and said, "Make ready 200 soldiers to go to Caesarea along with 70 horsemen and 200 spearmen by nine o'clock tonight, and provide mounts for Paul to ride so that he may be brought safely to Felix the governor." He wrote a letter that went like this:

Claudius Lysias to His Excellency Governor Felix, greetings. This man was seized by the Jews and they were about to kill him, when I came up with the detachment and rescued him because I had learned that he was a Roman citizen. Since I wanted to know what charge they were accusing him of, I brought him down to their council. I found he was accused with reference to controversial questions about their law, but no charge against him deserved death or imprisonment. When I was informed there would be a plot against this man, I sent him to you at once, also ordering his accusers to state their charges against him before you.

So the soldiers, in accordance with their orders, took Paul and brought him to Antipatris during the night. The next day they let the horsemen go on with him, and they returned to the barracks. When the horsemen came to Caesarea and delivered the letter to the governor, they also presented Paul to him. When the governor had read the letter, he asked what province he was from. When he learned that he was from Cilicia, he said, "I will give you a hearing when your accusers arrive too." Then he ordered that Paul be kept under guard in Herod's palace.

CHAPTER 24

THE ACCUSATIONS AGAINST PAUL

After five days the high priest Ananias came down with some elders and an attorney named Tertullus, and they brought formal charges against Paul to the governor. When Paul had been summoned, Tertullus began to accuse him, saying, "We have experienced a lengthy time of peace through your rule, and reforms are being made in this nation through your foresight. Most excellent Felix, we acknowledge this everywhere and in every way with all gratitude. But so that I may not delay you any further, I beg you to hear us briefly with your customary graciousness. For we have found this man to be a troublemaker, one who stirs up riots among all the Jews throughout the world, and a ringleader of the sect of the Nazarenes. He even tried to desecrate the temple, so we arrested him. When you examine him yourself, you will be able to learn from him about all these things we are accusing him of doing." The Jews also joined in the verbal attack, claiming that these things were true.

PAUL'S DEFENSE BEFORE FELIX

When the governor gestured for him to speak, Paul replied, "Because I know that you have been a judge over this nation for many years, I confidently make my defense. As you can verify for yourself, not more than 12 days ago I went up to Jerusalem to worship. They did not find me arguing with anyone or stirring up a crowd in the temple courts or in the synagogues or throughout the city, nor can they prove to you the things they are accusing me of doing. But I confess this to you, that I worship the God of our ancestors according to the Way (which they call a sect), believing everything that is according to the law and that is written in the prophets. I have a hope in God (a hope that these men themselves accept too) that there is going to be a resurrection of both the righteous and the unrighteous. This is the reason I do my best to always have a clear conscience toward God and toward people. After several years I came to bring to my people gifts for the poor and to present offerings, which I was doing when they found me in the temple, ritually purified, without a crowd or a disturbance. But there are some Jews from the province of

Asia who should be here before you and bring charges, if they have anything against me. Or these men here should tell what crime they found me guilty of when I stood before the council, other than this one thing I shouted out while I stood before them: 'I am on trial before you today concerning the resurrection of the dead.'"

Then Felix, who understood the facts concerning the Way more accurately, adjourned their hearing, saying, "When Lysias the commanding officer comes down, I will decide your case." He ordered the centurion to guard Paul, but to let him have some freedom, and not to prevent any of his friends from meeting his needs.

PAUL SPEAKS REPEATEDLY TO FELIX

Some days later, when Felix arrived with his wife Drusilla, who was Jewish, he sent for Paul and heard him speak about faith in Christ Jesus. While Paul was discussing righteousness, self-control, and the coming judgment, Felix became frightened and said, "Go away for now, and when I have an opportunity, I will send for you." At the same time he was also hoping that Paul would give him money, and for this reason he sent for Paul as often as possible and talked with him. After two years had passed, Porcius Festus succeeded Felix, and because he wanted to do the Jews a favor, Felix left Paul in prison.

CHAPTER 25

PAUL APPEALS TO CAESAR

Now three days after Festus arrived in the province, he went up to Jerusalem from Caesarea. So the chief priests and the most prominent men of the Jews brought formal charges against Paul to him. Requesting him to do them a favor against Paul, they urged Festus to summon him to Jerusalem, planning an ambush to kill him along the way. Then Festus replied that Paul was being kept at Caesarea, and he himself intended to go there shortly. "So," he said, "let your leaders go down there with me, and if this man has done anything wrong, they may bring charges against him."

After Festus had stayed not more than eight or ten days among them, he went down to Caesarea, and the next day he sat on the judgment seat and ordered Paul to be brought. When he arrived, the Jews who had come down from Jerusalem stood around him, bringing many serious charges that they were not able to prove. Paul said in his defense, "I have committed no offense against the Jewish law or against the temple or against Caesar." But Festus, wanting to do the Jews a favor, asked Paul, "Are you willing to go up to Jerusalem and be tried before me there on these charges?" Paul replied, "I am standing before Caesar's judgment seat, where I should be tried. I have done nothing wrong to the Jews, as you also know very well. If then I am in the wrong and have done anything that deserves death, I am not trying to escape dying, but if not one of their charges against me is true, no one can hand me over to them. I appeal to Caesar!" Then, after conferring with his council, Festus replied, "You have appealed to Caesar; to Caesar you will go!"

FESTUS ASKS KING AGRIPPA FOR ADVICE

After several days had passed, King Agrippa and Bernice arrived at Caesarea to pay their respects to Festus. While they were staying there many days, Festus explained Paul's case to the king to get his opinion, saying, "There is a man left here as a prisoner by Felix. When I was in Jerusalem, the chief priests and the elders of the Jews informed me about him, asking for a sentence of condemnation against him. I answered them that it was not the custom of the Romans to hand over anyone before the accused had met his accusers face-to-face and had been given an opportunity to make a defense against the accusation. So after they came back here with me, I did not postpone the case, but the next day I sat on the judgment seat and ordered the man to be brought. When his accusers stood up, they did not charge him with any of the evil deeds I had suspected. Rather they had several points of disagreement with him about their own religion and about a man named Jesus who was dead, whom Paul claimed to be alive. Because I was at a loss how I could investigate these matters, I asked if he were willing to go to Jerusalem and be tried there on these charges. But when Paul appealed to be kept in custody for the decision of His Majesty the Emperor, I ordered him to be kept under guard until I could send him to Caesar." Agrippa said to Festus, "I would also like to hear the man myself." "Tomorrow," he replied, "you will hear him."

PAUL BEFORE KING AGRIPPA AND BERNICE

So the next day Agrippa and Bernice came with great pomp and entered the audience hall, along with the senior military officers and the prominent men of the city. When Festus gave the order, Paul was brought in. Then Festus said, "King Agrippa, and all you who are present here with us, you see this man about whom the entire Jewish populace petitioned me both in Jerusalem and here, shouting loudly that he ought not to live any longer. But I found that he had done nothing that deserved death, and when he appealed to His Majesty the Emperor, I decided to send him. But I have nothing definite to write to my lord about him. Therefore I have brought him before you all, and especially before you, King Agrippa, so that after this preliminary hearing I may have something to write. For it seems unreasonable to me to send a prisoner without clearly indicating the charges against him."

CHAPTER 26

PAUL OFFERS HIS DEFENSE

So Agrippa said to Paul, "You have permission to speak for yourself." Then Paul held out his hand and began his defense:

"Regarding all the things I have been accused of by the Jews, King Agrippa, I consider myself fortunate that I am about to make my defense before you today, because you are especially familiar with all the customs and controversial issues of the Jews. Therefore I ask you to listen to me patiently. Now all the Jews know the way I lived from my youth, spending my life from the beginning among my own people and in Jerusalem. They know because they have known me from time past, if they are willing to testify, that according to the strictest party of our religion, I lived as a Pharisee. And now I stand here on trial because of my hope in the promise made by God to our ancestors, a promise that our 12 tribes hope to attain as they earnestly serve God night and day. Concerning this hope the Jews are accusing me, Your Majesty! Why do you people think it is unbelievable that God raises the dead? Of course, I myself was convinced that it was necessary to do many things hostile to the name of Jesus the Nazarene. And that is what I did in Jerusalem: Not only did I lock up many of the saints in prisons by the authority I received from the chief priests, but I also cast my vote against them when they were sentenced to death. I punished them often in all the synagogues and tried to force them to blaspheme. Because I was so furiously enraged at them, I went to persecute them even in foreign cities.

"While doing this very thing, as I was going to Damascus with authority and complete power from the chief priests, about noon along the road, Your Majesty, I saw a light from heaven, brighter than the sun, shining everywhere around me and those traveling with me. When we had all fallen to the ground, I heard a voice saying to me in Aramaic, 'Saul, Saul, why are you persecuting me? You are hurting yourself by kicking against the goads.' So I said, 'Who are you, Lord?' And the Lord replied, 'I am Jesus whom you are persecuting. But get up and stand on your feet, for I have appeared to you for this reason, to designate you in advance as a servant and witness to the things you have seen and to the things in which I will appear to you. I will rescue you from your own people and from the Gentiles, to whom I am sending you to open their eyes so that they turn from darkness to light and from the power of Satan to God, so that they may receive forgiveness of sins and a share among those who are sanctified by faith in me.'

"Therefore, King Agrippa, I was not disobedient to the heavenly vision, but I declared to those in Damascus first, and then to those in Jerusalem and in all Judea, and to the Gentiles, that they should repent and turn to God, performing deeds consistent with repentance. For this reason the Jews, after they seized me while I was in the temple courts, were trying to kill me. I have experienced help from God to this day, and so I stand testifying to both small and great, saying nothing except what the prophets and Moses said was going to happen: that the Christ was to suffer and be the first to rise from the dead, to proclaim light both to our people and to the Gentiles."

As Paul was saying these things in his defense, Festus exclaimed loudly, "You have lost your mind, Paul! Your great learning is driving you insane!" But Paul replied, "I have not lost my mind, most excellent Festus, but am speaking true and rational words. For the king knows about these things, and I am speaking freely to him because I cannot believe that any of these things has escaped his notice, for this was not done in a corner. Do you believe the prophets, King Agrippa? I know that you believe." Agrippa said to Paul, "In such a short time are you persuading me to become a Christian?" Paul replied, "I pray to God that whether in a short or a long time not only you but also all those who are listening to me today could become such as I am, except for these chains."

So the king got up, and with him the governor and Bernice and those sitting with them, and as they were leaving they said to one another, "This man is not doing anything deserving death or imprisonment." Agrippa said to Festus, "This man could have been released if he had not appealed to Caesar."

CHAPTER 27

PAUL AND COMPANY SAIL FOR ROME

When it was decided we would sail to Italy, they handed over Paul and some other prisoners to a centurion of the Augustan Cohort named Julius. We went on board a ship from Adramyttium that was about to sail to various ports along the coast of the province of Asia and put out to sea, accompanied by Aristarchus, a Macedonian from Thessalonica. The next day we put in at Sidon, and Julius, treating Paul kindly, allowed him to go to his friends so they could provide him with what he needed. From there we put out to sea and sailed under the lee of Cyprus because the winds were against us. After we had sailed across the open sea off Cilicia and Pamphylia, we put in at Myra in Lycia. There the centurion found a ship from Alexandria sailing for Italy, and he put us aboard it. We sailed slowly for many days and arrived with difficulty off Cnidus. Because the wind prevented us from going any farther, we sailed under the lee of Crete off Salmone. With difficulty we sailed along the coast of Crete and came to a place called Fair Havens that was near the town of Lasea.

CAUGHT IN A VIOLENT STORM

Since considerable time had passed and the voyage was now dangerous because the fast was already over, Paul advised them, "Men, I can see the voyage is going to end in disaster and great loss not only of the cargo and the ship, but also of our lives." But the centurion was more convinced by the captain and the ship's owner than by what Paul said. Because the harbor was not suitable to spend the winter in, the majority decided to put out to sea from there. They hoped that somehow they could reach Phoenix, a harbor of Crete facing southwest and northwest, and spend the winter there. When a gentle south wind sprang up, they thought they could carry out their purpose, so they weighed anchor and sailed close along the coast of Crete. Not long after this, a hurricane-force wind called the northeaster blew down from the island. When the ship was caught in it and could not head into the wind, we gave way to it and were driven along. As we ran under the lee of a small island called Cauda, we were able with difficulty to get the ship's boat under control. After the crew had hoisted it aboard, they used supports to undergird the ship. Fearing they would run aground on the Syrtis, they lowered the sea anchor, thus letting themselves be driven along. The next day, because we were violently battered by the storm, they began throwing the cargo overboard, and on the third day they threw the ship's gear overboard with their own hands. When neither sun nor stars appeared for many days and a violent storm continued to batter us, we finally abandoned all hope of being saved.

Since many of them had no desire to eat, Paul stood up among them and said, "Men, you should have listened to me and not put out to sea from Crete, thus avoiding this damage and loss. And now I advise you to keep up your courage, for there will be no loss of life among you, but only the ship will be lost. For last night an angel of the God to whom I belong and whom I serve came to me and said, 'Do not be afraid, Paul! You must stand before Caesar, and God has graciously granted you the safety of all who are sailing with you.' Therefore keep up your courage, men, for I have faith in God that it will be just as I have been told. But we must run aground on some island."

When the fourteenth night had come, while we were being driven across the Adriatic Sea, about midnight the sailors suspected they were approaching some land. They took soundings and found the water was twenty fathoms deep; when they had sailed a little farther they took soundings again and found it was fifteen fathoms deep. Because they were afraid that we would run aground on the rocky coast, they threw out four anchors from the stern and wished for day to appear. Then when the sailors tried to escape from the ship and were lowering the ship's boat into the sea, pretending that they were going to put out anchors from the bow, Paul said to the centurion and the soldiers, "Unless these men stay with the ship, you cannot be saved." Then the soldiers cut the ropes of the ship's boat and let it drift away.

As day was about to dawn, Paul urged them all to take some food, saying, "Today is the fourteenth day you have been in suspense and have gone without food; you have eaten nothing. Therefore I urge you to take some food, for this is important for your survival. For not one of you will lose a hair from his head." After he said this, Paul took bread and gave thanks to God in front of them all, broke it, and began to eat. So all of them were encouraged and took food themselves. (We were in all 276 persons on the ship.) When they had eaten enough to be satisfied, they lightened the ship by throwing the wheat into the sea.

PAUL IS SHIPWRECKED

When day came, they did not recognize the land, but they noticed a bay with a beach, where they decided to run the ship aground if they could. So they slipped the anchors and left them in the sea, at the same time loosening the linkage that bound the steering oars together. Then they hoisted the foresail to the wind and steered toward the beach. But they encountered a patch of crosscurrents and ran the ship aground; the bow stuck fast and could not be moved, but the stern was being broken up by the force of the waves. Now the soldiers' plan was to kill the prisoners so that none of them would escape by swimming away. But the centurion, wanting to save Paul's life, prevented them from carrying out their plan. He ordered those who could swim to jump overboard first and get to land, and the rest were to follow, some on planks and some on pieces of the ship. And in this way all were brought safely to land.

CHAPTER 28

PAUL ON MALTA

After we had safely reached shore, we learned that the island was called Malta. The local inhabitants showed us extraordinary kindness, for they built a fire and welcomed us all because it had started to rain and was cold. When Paul had gathered a bundle of brushwood and was putting it on the fire, a viper came out because of the heat and fastened itself on his hand. When the local people saw the creature hanging from Paul's hand, they said to one another, "No doubt this man is a murderer! Although he has escaped from the sea, Justice herself has not allowed him to live!" However, Paul shook the creature off into the fire and suffered no harm. But they were expecting that he was going to swell up or suddenly drop dead. So after they had waited a long time and had seen nothing unusual happen to him, they changed their minds and said he was a god.

Now in the region around that place were fields belonging to the chief official of the island, named Publius, who welcomed us and entertained us hospitably as guests for three days. The father of Publius lay sick in bed, suffering from fever and dysentery. Paul went in to see him and after praying, placed his hands on him and healed him. After this had happened, many of the people on the island who were sick also came and were healed. They also bestowed many honors, and when we were preparing to sail, they gave us all the supplies we needed.

PAUL FINALLY REACHES ROME

After three months we put out to sea in an Alexandrian ship that had wintered at the island and had the "Heavenly Twins" as its figurehead. We put in at Syracuse and stayed there three days. From there we cast off and arrived at Rhegium, and after one day a south wind sprang up and on the second day we came to Puteoli. There we found some brothers and were invited to stay with them seven days. And in this way we came to Rome. The brothers from there, when they heard about us, came as far as the Forum of Appius and Three Taverns to meet us. When he saw them, Paul thanked God and took courage. When we entered Rome, Paul was allowed to live by himself, with the soldier who was guarding him.

PAUL ADDRESSES THE JEWISH COMMUNITY IN ROME

After three days Paul called the local Jewish leaders together. When they had assembled, he said to them, "Brothers, although I had done nothing against our people or the customs of our ancestors, from Jerusalem I was handed over as a prisoner to the Romans. When they had heard my case, they wanted to release me because there was no basis for a death sentence against me. But when the Jews objected, I was forced to appeal to Caesar—not that I had some charge to bring against my own people. So for this reason I have asked to see you and speak with you, for I am bound with this chain because of the hope of Israel." They replied, "We have received no letters from Judea about you, nor have any of the brothers come from there and reported or said anything bad about you. But we would like to hear from you what you think, for regarding this sect we know that people everywhere speak against it."

They set a day to meet with him, and they came to him where he was staying in even greater numbers. From morning until evening he explained things to them, testifying about the kingdom of God and trying to convince them about Jesus from both the law of Moses and the prophets. Some were convinced by what he said, but others refused to believe. So they began to leave, unable to agree among themselves, after Paul made one last statement: "The Holy Spirit spoke rightly to your ancestors through the prophet Isaiah when he said,

'Go to this people and say,
"You will keep on hearing, but will never
 understand,
and you will keep on looking, but will
 never perceive.
For the heart of this people has become
 dull,
and their ears are hard of hearing,
and they have closed their eyes,
so that they would not see with their eyes
and hear with their ears
and understand with their heart
and turn, and I would heal them."'

"Therefore be advised that this salvation

from God has been sent to the Gentiles; they will listen!"

Paul lived there two whole years in his own rented quarters and welcomed all who came to him, proclaiming the kingdom of God and teaching about the Lord Jesus Christ with complete boldness and without restriction.